VICTOR HEADLEY

YARDIE

PAN BOOKS

First published 1992 by The X Press Limited

This paperback edition published 2017 by Pan Books
an imprint of Pan Macmillan
20 New Wharf Road, London N1 9RR
Associated companies throughout the world
www.panmacmillan.com

ISBN 978-1-5098-8269-4

Pan Macmillan does not have any control over, or any responsibility for,
any author or third-party websites referred to in or on this book.

1 3 5 7 9 8 6 4 2

A CIP catalogue record for this book is available from the British Library.

Printed and bound by CPI Group (UK) Ltd, Croydon, CR0 4YY

~r books
~iews and
~sletters
~ases.

This story is dedicated to Scorpion.
'Nuff respeck, Star!

The long line of passengers waiting to pass through the immigration control was noisy but colourful. After spending over eight hours in the skies, they were impatient. Anxious to get the formalities over with and meet their waiting families and friends. For many, it was the first time they had left Jamaica, arriving on the fabled shores of England, with their heads filled high with expectations. This year, an early spring had spread its warmth over the country. In the stuffy airport, those who had thought it wise to wear extra jumpers were visibly more restless than their fellow travellers.

Ten yards or so away from the immigration booth, a young man in a dark blue suit watched with interest as one of the officers questioned a newly arrived. He was too far away to hear the conversation but he got the gist of it from the passenger's gestures of indignation and the bits of sentences carried over by the man's booming voice.

'It's twelve years I don't see my sister, y'know. She send me the ticket . . . see the visa here! . . . Only a hundred pounds?! I don't come to stay, sah . . .'

Losing interest in the confrontation, D. unbuttoned his jacket and glanced around the airport arrival lounge. There was no other route to the exit fifty yards away. He breathed deeply and comforted himself with the thought that the returning resident's passport he was carrying should get him through without any problems. He had been briefed thoroughly by Skeets and knew his adopted life story by heart. The mission he was on was too important to too many people to leave anything to chance.

'Just play your part cool and ev'ryt'ing will be al'right,' Skeets had advised him.

D. left his thoughts to focus on his immediate situation. He was now next in line, after the voluminous woman now trying to convince a suspicious officer that she had, 'No intention to do any form of work in this country, sah.'

D. reached in his inside pocket and took out his passport. He adjusted his tie and picked up the leather case resting on the floor, and proceeded to the booth where the now available officer was beckoning him.

Standing before the white man with the thin ginger beard, he put down his case and sustained briefly the penetrating stare. The officer opened the British passport, looked at the photograph, then fixed D. once more.

'How long have you been away, sir?'

'I went to attend my mother's funeral. I spent six weeks there,' D. said in his best English.

The officer ran his pen along a list of names on the board in front of him, stopping half-way through.

'Miller . . . Miller . . . What is your date of birth, sir?'

D. didn't even blink. 'Twelfth of January 1957.'

The officer cast him a penetrating look, then scrutinized the photograph in front of him before closing the passport and nodding twice.

'Thank you, sir,' he said, handing D. the passport and turning towards the waiting queue.

D. took the document, picked up his case and walked towards the exit as normally as a returning resident would. He felt like jumping!

Fortunately he and Jonathan Miller looked somewhat alike. He hadn't bothered to enquire about the identity of

2

the passport's real owner; when you get offered the chance to travel to England for the first time . . . on a mission . . . you don't ask questions.

He followed the corridor, turned right at the end, and found himself walking alongside a waiting crowd leaning against the metal barriers that separated the public from the passengers. He relaxed as he walked amongst the other transatlantic passengers to the end of the lane, feeling confident about the rest of his plan. He had successfully played the part that had been set for him. Now it was his run. Though he was still unsure how he was going to make it work, he knew exactly what he wanted to do. He had spent the whole flight checking every aspect of the plan in his head.

It would be the biggest risk he had ever taken. That was no big deal. D. thought nothing of putting his life on the line. That's the way it had always been since he was old enough to make decisions himself. He'd put his life on the line for a hustle so many times that he saw losing it as an occupational hazard. He felt a tingling sensation in the pit of his stomach, as he did whenever danger was imminent.

As he got to the end of the barriers, he saw them. The two men were standing a little way back from the crowd, looking at him with the seemingly detached look that ghetto-born Jamaicans have developed as a survival shield. D. didn't recognize the faces, but there was no mistaking it was them. Skeets had explained that the two men who would meet him had been in the UK for several years, managing the outfit's operations. The older and taller of the two men gave D. a penetrating glance. He had a full-grown beard and a protruding stomach. Except for his eyes, which were threatening in their lack of expression, he looked like the gentle giant of children's story books. It was the shorter, smiling man with several large gold rings on his fingers who spoke first.

'Whapp'n, D., everyt'ing al'right?'

'Cool, you know.' D. nodded slowly, looking at each of his new friends in turn.

They walked towards one of the glass exit doors leading out of the airport lounge, D. in the middle. He felt as relaxed as a player with an extra ace up his sleeve. The silence lasted a few minutes until the short man said in a low voice: 'You know seh we supposed to take care ah de bizness, yeah?'

'I know ouno supposed to take me to a safe place,' D. replied, half-smiling. Then, more serious: 'First of all, I need to know who ouno is, seen? I can't trust anyone just so ah foreign, you know sah!'

The bearded giant stopped, a furious look on his face. 'Hey, bwoy, don't come cause no fuss y'hear! Jus' . . .'

'Cool nuh, Bigga. Mek we lef' yah first.' The other man stopped him, looking quickly around, anxious to avoid drawing attention to themselves. He seemed to be in command.

They went on through the exit, Bigga lagging slightly behind. The three men took the lift down to the car park, no one speaking a word. As they walked alongside the rows of parked cars, the short man took a bunch of keys out of his pocket, spinning it deftly around his finger. He finally turned into a parking bay and proceeded to open the door of a shiny blue Mercedes 350 sports model. He lifted up the seat to let D. climb into the back before sitting in the driver's seat and starting the engine. Bigga, meanwhile, shoved D.'s case into the boot and sat in the front.

The driver turned his head, staring at D. with a curious grin.

'OK, star, we know say you is a top soldier down ah Yard. But you see on yah, ah we run t'ings. We ah go look after you, man. Me name Joseph, seen? Skeets mus' ah tell you seh I would deal with you,' he said with a conciliatory tone.

'True.' D. looked straight at Joseph. 'Him also seh you would give me an apartment and the rest of my money.'

Joseph looked at Bigga and stared hard through the windscreen, before letting out a short laugh.

D. kept his composure. The half grin that slowly formed around the corner of his mouth led the two soldiers to believe he was only joking. Countless men, back in Jamaica, had learned too late that the grin was misleading: that far from joking, the grin gave notice that D. was deadly serious. But Bigga and Joseph weren't to know. They had been away from Yard too long, and weren't aware of his reputation in Kingston.

D. knew the two men had expected to have him 'under manners' from the start. Strictly speaking, Joseph was of higher rank than him in the order of the organization, and had naturally assumed that the newly arrived soldier would show him respect. He now realized that D. considered himself a *star*. He didn't mean much. The only respect D. ever showed was reserved for the few 'rudies' who had grown up and risked their lives with him back on the streets of West Kingston in his early days. Only a handful of living men fulfilled those requirements.

'So, what about the money, Joseph?' D. had spoken softly to mask the insistence of the demand. He wanted to find out just how hard these *ranks* were.

Joseph put the car into reverse and backed out of the parking bay before answering.

'You will get the money, me breddah, when we get to your apartment.' He stressed the last word with understated irony.

The Mercedes moved smoothly forward towards the slope leading to the parking exit. D. leaned back into the cosy leather seat and let the thumping bass from the speakers flow through him. Out of his window he could see rows of cars gliding alongside on the broad motorway, and pretty houses and fields beyond. The sun was bright and warm through the large windscreen, welcoming him to his new country.

According to the instructions he had been given, he was to let his contact, Joseph, handle the package he carried, enjoy his six weeks' stay in England, then return to Jamaica with the funds he would be given. A simple mission, but of the highest importance, he had been told.

Right now, spread out at the back of the expensive car, D. knew that he was in no hurry to get back to Jamaica and the hardship of day-to-day living in the ghetto. He was sure that he was at least as smart as Joseph; he could be running things here just as well. Besides, he had been doing a lot of thinking on the plane. He had flashed back to his early years on the streets; growing up. From school days in the poverty-stricken areas of downtown, dreaming of the big life he heard about from those who had managed to reach America, Canada, or England. He had waited for his break for years. The break out of the dusty, hungry streets and into the bright lights of big cities with their flash cars and large houses.

He began working for Skeets when he was about twelve years old; running errands, getting the odd dollar here and there, gradually learning the order of things in his part of town. Skeets was a big man in his area. He had taken a liking to the skinny, cocky kid who always offered to wash his car. In those days, D. thought that Skeets earned his living from the small rum bar he owned on West Avenue in Greenwich Farm. He found out later that there was much more to his mentor than met the eye. Skeets was well connected in America and travelled often, sometimes bringing back a pair of shoes or pants for D., clothes that the youngster would wear with great pride up and down the area.

D. had served his apprenticeship with zeal, showing himself to be reliable and fearless. He soon realized that he could make more money by working for the big shots downtown than he could ever earn in any of the dead-end trades his mother wished him to learn. As a consequence, he had deserted school early, concentrating instead on making a name for himself in West Kingston. He also discovered that he could get away with almost anything; very few boys were foolish enough to mess with him, knowing he was under Skeets' protection. As for the few who still dared to challenge him, they became the first victims of his tendency towards violence. Skeets had to call him to order more than once for using unnecessary violence against boys connected to *ranks* from other areas. Ruthlessness soon became synonymous with D.'s character.

He glanced at Joseph, casually steering the big car with one hand; the glitter of his rings and his fine, stylish clothes. Things definitely looked brighter on this side of the world. There was much money to be made here from someone as sharp as he was. He was sure about that.

Yes, he thought, smiling to himself, my time is well overdue.

They had reached what D. thought was the centre of

town. He could see all kinds of shops lining the street, with people everywhere. He looked with curiosity at the big double-decker red buses, similar to those on the postcard Donna had sent him.

'Is what area dis, star?' he asked above the music.

'Harlesden,' Joseph answered without turning around, 'we soon reach now.'

D. straightened himself on the seat. He looked attentively through the window, trying to get his bearings. He saw a group of nice-looking girls in front of a shop and kept his eyes on them while the car stopped at a traffic light. One of the girls met his intense gaze with an inviting smile. As the car moved forward, he smiled back at her and continued watching through the rear window until he could no longer see her. He leaned back in his seat feeling comfortable about the future. The Mercedes took a right turn from the main street and, after a few hundred yards, stopped smoothly alongside a row of three-storey houses. Joseph switched off the engine and got out of the car, followed by D. Bigga got out on the other side and took the suitcase out of the boot. D. stretched himself in the morning sun, looking around him at the neatly kept hedges, the tall flower pots and ornaments in the front garden of every house.

Joseph led the way past the gate and up the concrete stairs to the front door of a tall house. He opened it with his key and stepped into the corridor, followed by D., while Bigga locked the door behind him. They entered a flat through a door on the right, then down a flight of wooden stairs into a well-furnished living room. D. cast an admiring glance at the comfortable leather three-piece suite, the low smoked-glass coffee table, the polished wooden dining suite and the big-screen television with video recorder.

8

'Dis is your place, star?' he asked Joseph.

'True, you like it?'

The short man was sitting on the sofa, while Bigga had lodged his big frame into one of the leather chairs. D. eased himself into another chair before replying.

'Yes, man. So, is whe me ah go stay?'

Joseph looked at him with that enigmatic smile D. had learned to dislike in the short time he had known the older man. It seemed as if the man was making fun of him, or knew something which gave him an advantage. D. stared hard at Joseph and decided that the man reminded him of one of those *samfi* – the pseudo-obeah workers who cheat credulous country folks of their hard-earned money back home.

'I have one room in yah specially for you, man.' Joseph switched to business. 'So is weh de load deh, sah?'

D. looked at each of the two men in turn, equally enigmatic.

'I is a very expensive man right now, 'nuff English pounds dis worth.'

He got up, took off his jacket, and slowly unbuttoned his shirt.

Lifting up his vest, he unclipped a leather belt from around his stomach and pulled it around his body with his left hand. Closely watched by Bigga and Joseph, he slid a three-compartment plastic pouch alongside the belt and tossed it casually on the glass table.

Joseph reached over and took hold of the package. His hand went behind him to his hip pocket, from which he pulled out a wooden-handle ratchet knife. He flashed it open with consummate dexterity and, while holding the pouch in his left hand, proceeded to make a small cut through the several layers of plastic. Slowly, he drew out the shiny blade, a tiny mound of white powder balanced on the tip of it. He examined it closely before lifting the knife up to his face and tasting the powder with his tongue. He chewed for a few seconds, his face showing no expression, then smiling, he turned to Bigga.

'Yeah, top-grade stuff, man.'

Bigga nodded knowingly, still silent.

'Strictly the best, me boss,' D. said smiling, proud of the quality of the merchandise he had brought over.

'So wha', you a draw too?' Joseph enquired.

'When me ready,' D. lied.

Joseph flashed the knife shut and slipped it back into his pocket. He squinted in D.'s direction.

'Skeets seh is one ki you bring, weh de rest deh?'

'This bag is half a ki, me have the same amount right yah so.' D. patted the front of his trousers. 'Dem deh man strap me good, sah. Mek I gwan take it out.'

'The bathroom upstairs,' Joseph said. He turned to Bigga. 'Phone Lefty, tell him seh we ready fe him now.'

The big man got up and walked to the phone near the TV set. Meanwhile, Joseph headed for the kitchen to fetch his scales.

D. got up and climbed the stairs to the first floor. He found the bathroom on the left and was about to enter when he stopped, his eyes fixed on the entrance door five yards away. His mind was ticking over fast; he knew what he wanted to do but was still searching deep inside himself for a reason not to do it.

'It's now or never,' he thought, licking his lips.

He pulled the bathroom door closed. He could hear the two men exchanging remarks downstairs; he didn't have much time. Silently, D. walked to the door of the flat and unlocked the safety latch. He opened it slowly, praying the hinges wouldn't squeak, and stepped on to the landing. Carefully, he pulled the door shut behind him. His heart pumping in his chest, he proceeded to the street door, opening and closing it as silently as he could. Now, there was no turning back.

Outside, D. drew a sharp gulp of air and, stepping quickly down the concrete stairs, he passed the open gate and turned right on the street and into the midday sun.

Back in the living room, Joseph was busy setting up some meetings while Bigga checked carefully the exact weight of the merchandise, emptying each of the three compartments of the package in turn on to the scale plates. Joseph finally got off the phone and looked at the big man with a frown.

'Check wha' de bwoy ah do. Look like him get stuck up deh.'

Bigga left his work and climbed the stairs. He knocked loudly on the bathroom door, calling out. Suddenly suspicious, he tried the handle. The door opened on an empty room. The big man stood there for a few seconds, incredulous, before shouting to Joseph. 'Him gone, nobody nuh deh!'

Joseph rushed upstairs, running behind Bigga who was already outside. The two men stopped in front of the house, looking left and right. They stood there in silence for a moment then the big man erupted.

'I gawn kill that lickle raas!'

Bigga was in a fit of rage, throwing curses and loud expletives to the empty street. He couldn't believe that a 'bwoy' like D. would have the nerve to rob them. Joseph's face was like stone. He hadn't said a word, but the expression in his eyes spelled death.

'Come, man, we ha fe make some calls.' His voice was calm and controlled.

The two men walked back to the house silently. There would be no trial for an offence such as this one. The main

11

thing was to try and catch up with the fugitive before he could dispose of the stuff. After that it would be just a formality. No one had ever dared to pull a heist like this . . . They would make sure that the thief's punishment was a lesson to all. Besides, Joseph's reputation was at stake, both here and in Jamaica. D. had no place to run. Joseph was sure of that.

The top deck of the bus was only half full. D. looked absentmindedly at a gleaming green BMW in the showroom on the opposite side of the road. He was sitting at the back of the bus behind two black youths commenting excitedly on the music blaring out of their portable cassette player. The familiar pulse of the reggae rhythm penetrated his mind and he forced himself to relax.

He had paid his fare to the conductor after enquiring from one of the boys as to how to get to his destination. They told him he would have to change buses in order to reach East London. They'd let him know when to get off. Thankful for the help, D. drifted back to his meditation.

Once out of Joseph's house, he had run up to the High Street and boarded the first bus he saw. He knew he only had a few minutes before his hosts discovered his escape. Up to the moment when Joseph had tasted the merchandise, he was still unsure what to do. He didn't like the two men and he could see they were not going to treat him the way he expected. He thought of the consequences he would have to face; on the run from the posse in a strange land, with no back-up and no place to hide. He knew from the start that he was being used as a courier, nothing more, but his prime consideration had been to get out of Jamaica. It was only a matter of time before Lancey caught up with him and that was reason enough to leave the scene. He thought that he might find a way to set himself up once he arrived. Maybe work for the *ranks* who would meet him. He ruled this option out when they insulted him by treating him as a messenger boy. Either Joseph knew of him and had deliberately tried to *diss* him or Skeets had 'forgotten' to mention his background.

While he debated what to do in his mind, D. realized that he had a last chance to make a run for it. On his own turf he would have taken things in hand and taught these guys how to show respect to a *star* like himself. For the time being he only had one card to play and he wasn't going to waste it. Now, still loaded with almost a pound of first-grade base cocaine, he felt the excitement of danger in his spine. He knew that they would come after him and, knowing only too well the ruthlessness of his former bosses, he would have to use all his skills and experience to stay alive. The first thing he needed was a refuge, a safe place from where he would organize himself. After that, with some independent contacts to trade with and a few reliable soldiers, he felt he stood a good chance of making it.

'You get off here, boss.' The voice of the youth brought him back to the present. 'Any one of them two buses takes you to Hackney.'

D. thanked the two aspiring DJs and went down the stairs and off the bus. He followed a group of people who were boarding another red double-decker. Having paid his fare, he took a seat on the lower deck, half-way down the aisle. With a hiss and a roar of its engine, the bus joined the traffic.

His first impulse after his escape had been to head for Brixton and find Sammy. They had been friends from schooldays in Kingston, and D. knew he could count on him if in need. Sammy had left Jamaica to follow his mother to England years ago. He had returned for a short visit the previous year and given D. his address, the two young men still close, despite the time and distance between them. They still had that bond, that kind of deep loyalty, that binds together for life Jamaicans who have grown up in the same neighbourhood. Sammy had told him that he was working as a mechanic and now had a wife and three children. He lived in Brixton, because that was where you could find 'the most Yard man'. It was precisely that information which had made D. change his original plan; Brixton would be the first place they would expect him to show up. He was too smart to make such a mistake. Besides he didn't want to put Sammy in trouble.

D. knew that he would have to face Joseph and whoever else they sent after him, sooner or later, but he intended to pick the time and the place. He just needed a little time to set himself up for the showdown. Apart from Sammy, there was only one other unconnected person in the whole country who could help him out.

Donna had also left Jamaica several years earlier, one of her relatives having offered her the opportunity to travel to London to work in his catering enterprise. She and D. had ties which ran deep. Donna had been his first girl. Usually, the brief liaisons of childhood didn't count for much in the ghetto where young boys are only interested in *shegging* as many girls as possible. It's all part of growing up on the street, and feelings are not expected in those affairs. However, between Donna and D. it had been somehow different. Though they had both moved on to further relationships, the deep intimacy they had shared as youngsters, the *puppy love* that had brought them together in the first place, had never completely vanished. With time and experience, D. had come to realize that Donna was one of the few people he could safely trust.

She had shown on several occasions that she would

not hesitate to face danger on his behalf. He had never forgotten that. When he was on the run from a vengeful police officer whose brother he had badly beaten, Donna had hid him in her room in her mother's house until the search was over and he could make his way to the country to let things cool down for a while. The policeman, Lancey, was the most ruthless officer in the Jamaican police force. Known for his efficiency as a legal killer (*eradicator*), he would have punished Donna for hiding D., on top of exacting a vicious revenge on him.

Now, on the run in a strange land, D. knew she would do whatever she could to help him. Donna had never been back to the island, but had written him now and then, sending a card on his birthday, and twice even enclosing some English money. She had also written to inform him of the birth of her baby daughter four years before, and sent a picture of a small, dark and pretty thing – a miniature Donna.

The giggles and chatting of a group of schoolgirls behind him caught D.'s attention. He turned around and asked one of the girls: 'Which stop is it for Clapton?'

'The next one,' answered the girl, looking straight into his eyes. She was about fourteen, with plaited hair and a dark complexion.

'You know Redwald Road?' D. asked again, smiling.

The girl smiled back at him. 'Yeah, you have to turn right and walk down a little.'

The bus slowed down and stopped. The group of girls got out. D. followed them as they turned right, into a street bordered by blocks of low-rise flats. The girl who spoke to him on the bus lagged behind her friends. He caught up with her and walked side by side while the other girls gradually disappeared in the maze of alleyways between the blocks. After a while, the girl looked at him and asked, 'What area are you from?'

'I just come from Jamaica this morning. I'm looking for a friend who lives 'round here.'

The girl looked interested.

'Your parents Jamaican?' D. enquired.

'Yeah.'

'So wha', you been dere yet?' D. asked again.

'No. My aunty is going in December. She said she would take me,' the girl replied.

D. looked around him at the shops, the flats and the children playing on their way back from school. The scene was sunny and peaceful. He felt more relaxed now, walking in the bright afternoon with his guide. The girl told him that she lived not far from the address he was looking for. They crossed the road and walked through a large open space bordered by rows of nice, red-brick two-storey houses.

'What's your name?' the girl asked.

'Tony,' he lied, always cautious.

'My name is Sherry,' she said. The sideways glances she kept throwing in his direction had not gone unnoticed . . . She was pretty, but he was kind of busy for the time being. Later, maybe . . .

Sherry stopped in front of a long line of flats.

'The number you want is through that entrance,' she said, pointing at the porch facing them.

'Al'right, I'll find it now.' D. smiled at the girl. 'Thanks for the help.'

'OK, I'll see you another time.' Sherry walked away from him backwards, returning his smile. She spun around, and headed towards the street, turning back once more to wave at him.

D. walked up to the porch. The board near the staircase told him the number he was looking for was on the second floor. He climbed the stairs two at a time, wondering if he would be lucky enough to find Donna home. On the landing, he stopped in front of number 27 and knocked firmly twice on the wooden door. After waiting a while, he knocked again. Again there was no sign of life in the flat. He looked at his watch and reflected that Donna might be working, in which case he would have to wait her return.

He walked back downstairs. As he was still carrying the stuff on him, it was best to hang around until Donna eventually got home. He considered for a moment that she might have moved, but thought it unlikely as her last letter had arrived just six months ago. A group of children played football in front of the block. He called out to the goalkeeper, vigilantly guarding the area between two large metal bins.

'Skipper, any phone box around here?'

The freckled-faced kid took his eyes off the action for a moment.

'Yeah, there's one just behind the pub, down there.' He pointed towards some shops across a parking lot.

D. thanked him and headed for the precinct. He found the payphone and dipped in his trouser pockets for some change. He had spent his first English money on the plane to buy some duty-free cigarettes (which he had abandoned during his flight from Joseph's apartment, along with his jacket and luggage). Apart from the bus fares, he hadn't spent anything else from the £500 Skeets had given him. He put a 10p coin in the slot and dialled Sammy's number from memory. After a few seconds, someone picked up the phone.

'Allo,' a woman answered.

'Allo, could I speak to Sammy?'

'Sammy is at work. Who's speaking please?'

'My name is Tony. What time will he be back?'

'He should be in about seven.' The woman spoke a polite, straight English.

'OK, I'll call back.'

'Bye.'

D. left the telephone and walked back slowly by the shops, hands in his pockets. Unless he knew many Tonys, Sammy might remember the nickname D. had used back in their school days. He would be surprised to know he had reached England.

D. sat on a low wall near the parking lot. From there he could see the entrance to the flats. The football game had been interrupted by a heated dispute. A dozen players were huddled together, pushing, shoving and shouting at each other. He watched them with amusement for a while. As a youngster, he used to love football but then he got older and found that he had little time to play. He led a busy life.

On the landings of the block of flats, D. could see and hear the residents' daily life unfold. Neighbours chatting, women chasing little children to get them home; usual everyday scenes in Hackney. The dwellings didn't look new and the stairway and corridors were far from clean, but it was a long way from certain areas of West Kingston. This is what people called a 'poor' area in England, D. reflected. It wasn't that bad.

D. had waited about an hour monitoring all the comings and goings in the flat, when he caught a glimpse of a woman's silhouette coming from the side street. He couldn't make out the features yet, but the walk was unmistakable. The girl was now fifty yards or so away from him; as she turned left to walk through the porch, he smiled as he saw the still familiar profile of Donna. She didn't notice him. He waited until she had disappeared up the staircase before he got up and followed her. He heard her footsteps as he was climbing the stairs, and reached the first landing in time to see her turn up the second flight of stairs. He called out: 'Hey girl, weh you ah rush go so?'

The footsteps stopped.

'A who dat?' The voice expressed surprise.

Donna walked back down two steps. Her eyes met D.'s contented grin across the metal railing of the staircase. Her face broke into a wide smile.

'Lord! D., is you fe true?' she exclaimed, stepping towards him, arms open.

She hugged him, then, looking at him closely: 'Wait, you a grow beard now,' she quipped, passing her hand over the short stubble on his chin. 'Is when you reach, man? So why you never write tell me seh you coming?'

D. laughed at the flurry of questions. Donna held his arm, searching his eyes.

'Well, you know seh I don't really write letters. I just reach dis morning, you know,' he said.

She led him up the stairs, still looking at him with amazement. They walked up the landing to Donna's flat and entered. The place was nicely decorated and looked comfortable, with thick carpet on the floor.

'It look like you make it, Donna, man,' D. said, looking around the place.

'Well, I'm working now, so t'ings are not too bad,' she explained. 'Sit down nuh, man!'

He sat on the sofa, Donna beside him. She stared at him as he spoke, the way a mother tries to read beyond her child's words.

'So is holiday you come for, or you plan to settle on yah?' she enquired.

20

'I t'ink I'll stay for a while.' D. leant back on the sofa, grinning confidently. He stretched himself, then looking straight at Donna: 'I need you to help me. Me deh pon some serious business.'

'D., anyt'ing I can do for you, I will. You know dat.'

D. nodded, touched by the girl's unswerving loyalty. It was the same Donna, the same smile, the same feelings as when they had parted years before. He took her hand and held it lightly in his.

'You don't really change, miss. You got bigger though . . . The good life?' he said teasingly.

Donna laughed. She asked with a look of concern, 'Tell me somet'ing; you eat from you come?'

'To tell you the truth, the way t'ings happen I all forget about food,' D. replied, shaking his head.

'Al'right, you just relax here, I set up some dinner. We'll talk after.'

She got up, walked to the television set and switched it on, before disappearing in the kitchen. She came back after a few minutes and placed a glass of orange juice on the table in front of D.

'I can't believe you reach England.' Donna looked at him, still amazed. 'Lord! What a day.' She laughed as she returned to the kitchen.

D. stretched himself across the sofa and closed his eyes, oblivious to the murmur of the television. Everything was as he had hoped it would be. Despite his precarious position, he felt good within himself, as if luck was on his side. He had survived so many desperate situations back in his old neighbourhoods that he had come to be known as Lucky D. Even his enemies preferred to avoid a confrontation with him, because they believed he had some sort of jinx working for him.

Lying in Donna's comfortable sofa, he felt totally

secure. From this haven, hidden from the eyes of the ravenous crowd now looking for him, he would have time to get organized. He would have to find out if Donna had any contacts he could use, preferably unconnected to his former outfit. First, he would lie low for a while, to let the excitement die down. Then he would learn all there was to know about the 'English Connection' and its players. He had money to last him for a while; he didn't need to take unnecessary risks.

Thoughts and images unfolded in D.'s mind. All tension vanished from his body and he drifted into a light sleep.

'Wake up, man, dinner ready.'

Donna's voice and a gentle nudge brought D. out of his lethargic state. He opened his eyes and stretched. Donna had set a tray on the table, and the smell of the food was teasing his hungry stomach. He got up and headed for the bathroom, which she said was on the right in the corridor. There, he proceeded to unstrap himself from the belt that held his precious investment. He held the plastic package up for a moment with a satisfied look, then tucked it in his waist and pulled his shirt over his trousers. He washed his face and hands before going back to the living room.

Donna was still in the kitchen. D. took the package from his waist and pushed it down against the arm of the sofa. He sat, pulled the tray towards him and started to eat. She came in, carrying her dinner, and sat down beside him.

'So you still know how to cook Yard food,' he teased her.

'Den wha', you must t'ink seh me turn English girl,' she retorted.

They both laughed. They ate, watching the television. The meal over, Donna took the trays back to the kitchen while D. sat, sipping his orange juice. When she returned, he asked, 'Weh your pickney deh?'

'I leave her by my mother when I go to work,' she explained. 'I have to go pick her up soon.'

D. pointed to a framed picture on top of the TV. 'She look pretty though, and favour you too.'

Donna smiled. 'She will be five in July,' she said.

'So what happ'n to the baby father?' D. continued.

'Him deh ah jail . . . seven years fe killing a man in a dance.'

'So him a bad bwoy?'

Donna shrugged. 'Ah just foolishness really; him stab a man over some girl. Him might come out next year.' She didn't seem to be too bothered about the situation. 'I can't watch that D. Me and the pickney have to survive some way,' she added.

He nodded thoughtfully, then asked, 'Leroy over here, nuh true?'

'Yeah, him live not too far from here, you know.'

Leroy was Donna's older brother. He had managed to leave Jamaica the year after she did and had never been back. Although only two years older than D., Leroy was much bigger in size. He had made a name for himself back in the old days by beating up three would-be robbers single-handedly. D. realized quickly that the big boy would be a good ally to have. Particularly as they were somewhat related through Donna. At the beginning he had been cautious, unsure whether Leroy would approve of him checking his sister. In time, however, they had become

23

good friends, Leroy having proved to be a reliable help whenever he was in trouble.

'Leroy get married, you know, D. Him have three youths by one girl from on yah. Him open a record shop a few years back; dat keeps him busy,' Donna explained.

'So Leroy settled down . . .' D. said, amused.

Back in Kingston, Leroy had made some powerful enemies. Not that he was *bad* in the usual sense, but he was quick-tempered and didn't like being told what to do.

'So what about you, D.?' Donna had a serious look on her face. 'What you planning to do now? You said you had some business to do?'

D. stood her interrogating gaze for a while. Slipping his right hand down the side of the sofa, he brought out the plastic-wrapped parcel and placed it on the table.

'See me investment deh!' He looked at Donna, watching her reaction. She looked at the package, then at him.

'So is dat you ina now,' she said slowly. Her tone of voice was disapproving.

'You know how much money dis worth?' he asked.

Donna didn't answer, she was staring at the television.

'Whapp'n, you don't wan' me fe make it ina England?' He tried to sound convincing. 'Dat deh t'ing you see here gwan set me up one time, you know?'

Donna turned towards him. She looked sad rather than angry, her eyes hard into his.

'I want you to make it, yes. But this is not the way, D.' She pointed to the small plastic parcel on the table in front of them. 'This t'ing will only bring you trouble, pure trouble.'

D. squinted. He wanted her to see his point; there was no other way he could set himself up quickly in this new country.

'Hear wha'; I got lucky to come out of Jamaica. T'ings

got kinda hot fe me down dere. Right now, dis is my only chance and I not going to waste it. I don't have not'ing to lose.'

Donna sighed. The joy she felt at seeing him after all this time was now spoiled by the fear for his safety. She knew the kind of life people involved in that type of business led; on the run from the police, always watching over their shoulder, the violence, the madness. Deep inside she also knew there was no way she could change D.'s mind. He had always lived by his wits and had made himself a name. Nothing he could say however would allay her deep dislike of anything connected with drugs.

'You don't have to worry, Donna, man; I will look after you. Everyt'ing you need, and your pickney, I'll get it for you.'

'Look, I can't stop you, but I don't want not'ing to do with it. Don't deal with no business in here . . . That's all I'm asking you.'

'Don't worry about dat, Donna, let me take care of my runnin's, me an' you safe.' His voice grew softer, the way it used to years before. 'You know seh me check fe you, look how long I don't see you; we have better t'ings to do than fuss over dat, Donna.'

She looked at him, memories flashing through her mind. She felt the same about him as she did before, wanting to believe anything he said. She had never really cared for anyone but him. Slowly, as he took her hand and brought his face closer to hers, her fears vanished away. D. was back in her life.

he atmosphere was hot and smoky in the basement room. The set always played a revival selection in the early morning hours, to allow the dancers to cool off after the heavy dancehall music. Couples were lined up against the walls, tightly swaying to the rhythm of the Studio One bass line. Standing beside a speaker box, D. was busy drawing on a spliff of prime sensimillia. He and Leroy had arrived at the shebeen about two hours earlier. After spending some time near the bar, drinking beer with two of Leroy's associates, D. had chosen to settle in this corner opposite the door, from where he could see the entrance, through the corridor. The place was full almost every night, peaking at about five in the morning when all the ravers, hustlers, and players, all the regulars of the North London night scene had arrived.

High Noon, the top sound for the last three years, attracted so many people that it was often a problem to fit everyone in. Tonight, the two rooms and the corridor were full, with people rocking lazily in the confined space, amidst the sweat, perfume, and smoke. The overcrowding was too much to bear sometimes and, in the general state of intoxication from liquor and other substances, arguments and fights were not uncommon. Yet, no matter how crowded the place, no matter how long the queue outside, High Noon was a must for anyone involved in the night life. Only the mighty Jah Shaka could rival it.

D. first came to know the sound through Leroy who

had taken him there about a week after his arrival. He had gotten acquainted with a few of the DJs and usually spent some time at the shebeen most nights. It was a similar scene to the one he had left in Jamaica, except that there the dances were held outdoors. Recently settled Yardies were numerous in this part of London and kept the Jamaican-style sounds such as High Noon in business. Besides the Yardies who had obtained legal resident status, many had come into the country on a visitor's visa and simply 'extended' their stay, unofficially and indefinitely. For anyone coming from a poor background in Kingston's tenements, England, no matter how tight things were getting, was still a more comfortable environment to live in.

The high proportion of newly arrived Jamaican youths in the area had adversely affected the local hustlers; the competition was now tougher. Furthermore, the new-comers didn't operate by the same principles as their UK counterparts. They were totally ruthless; they didn't respect the established hierarchy, and were not prepared to allow anything like friendship or allegiances stand in their way. They were hungry, and wanted money. Lots of it, and now. As a result, in the last five years, the atmosphere in the area had become more tense, even more volatile, than before. The use of violence in settling 'trade' disputes had now become common practice.

D. took a deep draw from the spliff and glanced at the girl to his right. For the best part of an hour, she had been trying to attract his attention. She had asked him for a light twice. He didn't mind the attention but had played it cool so far. The girl was looking fine, about medium height and wearing a light-coloured dress. She had the sort of haircut that was in vogue for young Black women – short at the back. In the six weeks that he had been in England, D. had avoided getting involved with any of the local girls, spending his time between Donna's flat, the shebeen, and Leroy's record shop. He had made a few contacts which he cultivated cautiously; he didn't intend to sell the bulk of his merchandise until he had found a source of supply, one unconnected to his former outfit.

The Spicers had managed in the last two years to gain control of nearly all the channels feeding the Black community in London. They had also succeeded in setting up bases in several of the main country towns. In Manchester, Birmingham, and Bristol violent skirmishes had occurred between local 'soldiers' and the few independent dealers who still refused to pay dues to the organization.

D. had found himself an associate. Charlie had been in England less than two years but was already nicely set up. Leroy had introduced him to D., having explained that he wasn't connected in the drugs business, but that Charlie would help him. As it turned out, Leroy was right; Charlie was the right man to meet for someone newly arrived and independent. The tall brown-skinned man knew everything about the trade and everyone involved in it in town. At first, D. had treated him in a friendly but cautious manner. He was naturally suspicious, particularly because Charlie had previously lived in New York. He observed his new friend carefully for several weeks until, finally, he accepted that Charlie had started out in a very similar position to his own.

Having grown up from an early age in the Bedford-Stuyvesant area of New York, Charlie had found himself a virtual outsider on the London scene. After a while, he succeeded in setting up a chain of supplies that allowed him to make a name for himself; everyone knew now that Charlie's stuff was top quality. Nobody had forgotten either, the way he had dealt with two young Yardies who

28

had attempted to rob him one night outside the shebeen. After sticking a gun in his stomach and taking three ounces of cocaine from him, they had been foolish enough to hang around in the dance, getting high and boasting. They never really saw what happened . . . Charlie had walked in, found them amongst the dancers, and shot each one in turn, in the legs. He then coolly searched them, retrieved most of his property, and left the pair bleeding and groaning on the floor. Since that day, no one else had tried anything against him.

Charlie had politely but firmly rejected several offers from the Spicers to go into partnership. He had managed to keep them out of his business in New York and intended to do the same here.

D. and Charlie struck a closer friendship when they discovered that they had lived only a few streets from one another in Greenwich Farm, back in Jamaica. They were also about the same age.

Charlie was the kind of example D. planned to follow; he had a nice house, wore stylish clothes, and drove a new model black BMW. All this from starting out two years before with only one pound of Colombian cocaine out of New York!

D. finished the spliff and took a sip from his Budweiser. He knew that Charlie would show up sooner or later, but punctuality, a rare commodity amongst Jamaicans, was not one of his qualities.

Studio One selection after Studio One selection. The selector had the dancers where he wanted them, begging for more. Nobody who understood the history and roots of reggae could resist any record on the legendary Studio One label. From its Brentford Road headquarters in Kingston, Studio One and its founder Clement Dodd had encapsulated every form of reggae expression. His were the original bass lines, the original drum patterns still borrowed from heavily by contemporary reggae producers and US rappers. Somehow, no other rhythms in reggae seemed to swing as perfectly as a Studio One rhythm.

In response to the shouts of 'forward' and 'lift it up', the operator started the tune again from the top. The punch of the bass line got the couples straight back in the groove.

D. looked to his right; the girl in the white dress was rocking slowly, arms outstretched and head bowed, enjoying every beat of the music. He reached out and touched her left arm. The girl raised her head, her eyes searching his before she stepped towards him. He held her waist lightly in his right arm and they started rocking, tuning to each other's slow gyrations. He could feel the girl's face tight against his and her hands holding him lightly. She was a good dancer, following him around the beat, answering every slight move of his hips with a slight sway of her own. The song finished.

'Dat tune yah short,' he whispered in the girl's ear before letting go of her.

She smiled at him, staying close. Her eyes were slightly slanted, her skin a shiny dark brown hue. D. smiled back. As the beat of the next song surged from the speakers, she came against him of her own accord and put her arms around his shoulders. They began to sway together, slower and tighter this time. They rocked through two more tunes, exchanging few words, absorbed in the rhythm patterns of their welded bodies. Then the selector decided to change the mood. The heavy thump of a ragamuffin bass line shook the crowd, couples let go of each other and before long the whole venue was stepping and jumping wildly.

D. and his partner started to dance side by side. She

had told him her name was Jenny. The music was stirring the dancers into a frenzy, the beat bouncing from wall to wall. As the tune ended and another hot rhythm began to pound, he leaned towards her.

'Go and buy some drinks for you and your friend, and get me a Budweiser,' he said in her ear, handing her a £10 note.

Jenny took the money and headed for the bar. D. peeled off some sheets of Rizla paper and was about to build a spliff when he saw them. Against the opposite wall, near the door, he recognized the face of the tall, dark youth who had been watching him for several nights. Wearing a white Kangol flat cap and half hidden by rows of dancers, he was staring at D. intensely. His partner, a shorter man with a near-shaven head and sporting several large gold chains, was leaning against the door, sipping from a bottle.

D. proceeded to build his spliff, slowly sticking the paper together, apparently oblivious to the two pairs of eyes fixed on him. They had a certain attitude about them, which suggested who they were even before D. enquired about them. Charlie had told him that the taller one with the dead face was Blue, a soldier for the Spicers who had settled in England five years ago. Alfie, his companion, was the brother of a Miami *ranks*, something of a singer, and a show-off.

Charlie had dismissed Alfie as an 'idiot', but told D. to watch out for Blue; he was an experienced knifeman, a bad *bwoy* from his early days in the Waterhouse area of Kingston. He was known for his lack of humour and his inclination towards violence.

D. lit up the spliff, his mind alert while he blew out a cloud of smoke with apparent nonchalance. He knew the two soldiers wouldn't make a move until they had orders to do so. He also knew that as much as Joseph wanted him dead, he also needed to take the rest of the merchandise from him. He just had to stay on his guard until they made their move.

Anyone associated with D. was bound to become a target eventually, but Charlie didn't mind that. He had listened to D.'s story and, concluding that it was a smart move, had elected to stick by his new friend through trouble. Besides, Charlie had no love for the Spicers, suspecting them of having been behind the robbery attempt on him the year before.

Jenny came back with the drinks. D. opened the can, took a sip of the beer, and placed it on the speaker box next to him. He was keeping an eye on the two men across the room, while talking in Jenny's ear. They were getting on fine; D. found that she was easy to talk to and seemed to like him. She wasn't stuck up in the way he had been told many English-born girls were.

He was telling Jenny how pretty he thought she was when, from the corner of his eye, he saw Blue making his way through the crowd towards him. His smile vanished and his face became expressionless, as he felt the surge of energy through his body. Without a word, he pulled Jenny gently but firmly backwards, placing her behind him. The girl noticed the change in him and didn't ask any questions. Slowly, D. took the ratchet knife from his back pocket and dropped his hands loosely by his side. He saw Leroy talking to a friend near the bar ten yards away. D. took his breath and blew the air through his mouth, slowly. He was ready.

Blue was coming right at him. A sharp flick of the wrist; the blade of D.'s knife was out. Two yards in front of him, Blue stopped. Two pairs of steely eyes locked into each other, a silent duel . . .

'My boss wan' fe talk,' Blue said after a few tense seconds, making himself heard over the din of the music.

Suddenly there was space around the two men. Even for those who didn't know anything about them, it was plain to see that some kind of confrontation was at hand.

'I don't need fe talk to nobody,' D. retorted sharply. He didn't want this conversation to last too long.

Blue looked down, and then straight back into D.'s eyes. Stone-faced he delivered his message.

'Star, hear wha' now . . . I supposed to arrange a meeting. Any time, any place.'

D.'s brain was working fast. He knew that, one way or another, they would try to set him up. This was the first play and he had to be sharp.

'Tell your boss I'm not interested. The way I see it, dem owe me. Mek we call it quit, seen?!'

Blue's face broke into a vicious grin. He nodded slowly, then the frozen look reappeared.

'I will give dem your answer.' The voice was like the face – cold. He turned and walked back into the crowd. D. watched him make his way out the door followed by his accomplice. Slowly, he closed the blade of the knife and slipped it back in his pocket. With the 'meeting' now over, the dancers had reclaimed the dance space around him. No one in their right mind hung around in this type of situation; innocent casualties all too often resulted from dancehall fights. The music hadn't stopped pumping. Only the subtle change of atmosphere had warned those in the close vicinity of the challenge of the impending danger.

Jenny was back by D.'s side. She observed him, unsure whether she should ask him about the incident. Yet he seemed relaxed, sipping his drink slowly. He turned to her with the mischievous grin which was one of his trademarks.

'I t'ink seh you gone,' he said in her ear.

'What was that about?' she ventured, half expecting a scolding reply.

But he didn't mind her question.

'Jus' business, man. Everyt'ing cool.'

She looked into his face, serious, but decided against questioning him further and simply shook her head to let him know that she didn't believe that everything was 'cool'.

He took hold of her arm and pulled her closer to him. He whispered in her ear.

'So wha' happ'n, I hope seh me an' you still nice, 'cause I really like you, you know.'

She didn't answer. She simply stood right against him, listening to his voice softly speaking. He still felt the rush of adrenalin in his body, the unspent tension of the encounter pulsating in his veins. He held on to Jenny while keeping a discreet watch on the movements in the room.

The corridor was crowded with recently arrived ravers trying to slip into the room. The dance was now in full swing, the air heavy with heat and smoke. Right across the room, D. saw a familiar head amongst a mass of people. Charlie was looking around the room from the door, probably trying to locate him. D. saw him exchange a few words with a youth in a blue silk shirt by the entrance then push his way through the sweating crowd. He knew exactly where to find D., shoving people aside as he made his way to the back wall. Charlie finally reached his destination, the large rope chain around his neck gleaming against his white sweater in the darkness.

'Yes, Don!' D. greeted him, gently pulling Jenny to the side.

'What's happening, D.?' Charlie grinned, his eyes half

closed. Leaning closer he said, 'I have something for you, let's step out.'

D. nodded.

'Wait here, baby, I soon come,' he said in Jenny's ear, before following Charlie.

They walked through the crowd, stepping on a few toes before reaching the door. Charlie had signalled to the youth in the blue shirt, who was now following them. They got out of the house, down the steps, and started to walk up the street.

The night was mild, alive with the sound of reggae music blaring out of the rows of parked cars. Small groups of people, some cooling out from the dance, some just arrived, were hanging around on the pavement.

Charlie stopped by his BMW and turned towards D.

'This is my cousin Mickey,' he said. 'Him come over last year.'

D. looked at the lanky figure dressed in blue silk and nodded. The youth stood his stare briefly.

'Respect, D.,' he said.

D. took in the dark features, the sharp cut on the left cheek, trying to recall where he knew Mickey from. He never forgot a face, no matter how long it was since he hadn't seen it.

'Is which part you from, star?' he finally asked.

Mickey was standing still, slouched to the left against the side of the car. As Charlie got into the driver's seat he said, 'Maxfield Avenue.'

D. knew who the youth was before he had finished speaking.

Mickey went around the car and opened the passenger door. He lifted up the seat and got in the back, pulling the seat back into position. D. got in the front seat and closed the door.

'We have some important business to deal with,' Charlie started. 'Things come through today.'

D. stopped him. 'Hold on, supa.'

He turned towards Mickey in the back seat, looking at him intensely. 'You name Sticks?'

It wasn't a question. The youth nodded gravely. 'True,' he answered.

There was silence in the car for a few seconds. Then a puzzled Charlie asked, 'Wait, you know my cousin?'

Sticks . . . Maxfield Avenue . . . Jerry . . . Memories started to flow through D.'s mind. He remembered the youth well, from five years before.

Sticks was only about thirteen at the time; he was one of a group of youngsters Jerry had tried to prevent from turning bad. Jerry Dread, as everyone called him, was D.'s older brother. He had taught him much of what he knew about survival on the streets. Jerry himself had started out early, and earned a reputation as a tough youth in the Kingston 13 area. At eighteen years of age, he was a tall, well-built young man with a fearless disposition and self-assured ways.

He had good contacts and, with a little sponsorship, was going to become one of the top men in his neighbourhood. It was about that time that Jerry, to everyone's surprise, had turned away from a future as a *ranks* and become a Rasta.

At first, people thought it was only a cosmetic change and that he would soon be back to his rough ways. However, Jerry underwent a complete transformation, reading the Scriptures, praising Jah, and declaring he was now serving Selassie, Emperor of Ethiopia. He spent most of his time in the company of older dreads, disappearing for long spells in the Bull Bay area of St Andrews.

To D., the whole thing was simply amazing. Aged

36

fifteen at the time, he couldn't quite grasp all the elements of Black history and culture that Jerry was continually passing on to him, but he could feel in his brother an inner peace that wasn't there before.

D. loved his older brother, and this newly found faith made him idolize him even more. He started growing locks also, much to their mother's dismay. She didn't approve of Jerry's hairstyle, being a fervent Methodist Christian, but she was glad to see a change for the better in her son's attitude. They didn't see eye to eye on religious matters, but there was nothing between them that the love they had for each other couldn't overcome.

Soon the 'new' Jerry had moved to Maxfield Avenue with a pretty girl who had given him a baby daughter. He had also taken a job as a mechanic. In his new area, Jerry quickly became a personality. He was loved by all, young and old. He always took time to talk to elderly neighbours, occasionally giving them a helping hand when needed. Many youngsters in the vicinity had also started to visit Jerry. They loved to hear him speak of Africa, Marcus Garvey, and the achievements of Black people throughout history. Also, if any of them was hungry, the young dread would always find something for him to eat. His ways were something of an exception in the harsh West Kingston neighbourhood where taking was the norm and giving a rare occurrence.

Gradually, Jerry gained the respect of even the toughest residents of Maxfield Avenue. When not working, he could usually be found sitting on a stool in the courtyard of his house, surrounded by an assorted crowd, reasoning about the Bible. He also encouraged the youths to learn a trade and tried to get them involved in some craft, holding improvised woodwork, painting, or mechanic workshops . . . open to all.

Sticks' mother lived a few streets away from Jerry's house and consequently, the bony boy had become a regular in the yard. At first, he only came to see what he could exploit the kind dread, as most youths did. After a while however, he began to seek Jerry's advice on various problems and generally enjoying his company.

Sticks' own older brother had been in prison for several years and his father was living in America. He needed a model, someone to look up to, someone to make sense of the deprivation around him. He was still inclined to act rashly at times and tended to neglect school, but behind the tough streetwise façade, Jerry could feel that the boy was intelligent and had potential. He just needed direction to escape the vicious circle of poverty and crime. Had he lived, Jerry might have made a difference for Sticks and a few other youths in the area.

Drawing a long breath, D. snapped out of his meditation and said to Charlie, 'I know dat youth deh long time, me breddah.'

For a few short seconds, Charlie saw a mixture of pain and anger on D.'s face. He didn't ask anything else and got back to business.

'Al'right, my merchandise reached today, top quality, man.'

'Nice work.' D. smiled.

'Right now, we're gonna get into production. We can make much more by setting up some houses and dealing direct. We ain't gonna let them guys control the whole market; if we organize properly, we can keep a lot of the action.'

Charlie outlined his plan with conviction. He was serious about his business and had already explained the deal to D. a few days before.

Basically he wanted to start retailing instead of just

supplying raw material to dealers who then processed it and made a maximum profit at street level.

'The way things run now, we take the most risks and let the dealers make all the money. That was OK before, when I was working alone. Right now, all we have to do is set up maybe two houses first where we can make wash-rock. We need one security team for each house, plus some collectors to distribute to the dealers and pick up the cash from them. That way, we reduce the chances of getting busted by not selling from the production houses. Even the dealers won't know where we are based.'

Charlie calmly explained the scenario to D. He had done a lot of thinking and all the details were taken care of. It was a master plan which he had been waiting to implement.

As he hadn't been able to trust anyone since coming in the country, he had had to restrict himself to a small piece of the action. Yet now things had changed. Together with D. they could expand, make much more money and faster. Of course, that would mean taking over customers and territory that at present belonged to the Spicers.

'What I'm thinking of is this . . . I got two kis this morning, if you put your stuff on top, we can turn enough crack to pay everybody, make the next buy, and still get a good profit.'

D. liked what he was hearing. It sounded sensible and very rewarding. He grinned.

'Yeah, man, I love dem way deh. One t'ing though, if we going to take over the market, we gonna need a serious security team. Shots bound fe lick.'

'I thought of that too.' Charlie smiled confidently. 'Mickey here will control the retailing operations with his crew. I know some good chemists and I started checking some soldiers. All we have to do is to supervise the whole thing and make sure the supplies come in regularly. My sources are safe and we can use my couriers to start with.'

Charlie leaned back in the leather seat. Judging by his eyes, he was still on a high, but his plan was a brilliant one. Charlie took cocaine regularly, he had done so for several years. He seemed to know his limits though and didn't overdo it. He was a rare exception; most consumers aim to take as much as possible, to remain spaced out through the day. As the high of a crack 'hit' only lasted a short time, this meant smoking the pipe as often as possible, as long as the money lasted. Of course, that required a rather large income, earned either from trading or various other dubious means. Very few people involved in the scene had regular jobs!

Sticks had been sitting at the back, motionless, listening attentively to Charlie's plan. He wanted to work with his cousin who had promised him some good earnings. Since arriving from Kingston the previous year, he had survived by doing small things here and there, learning to move about in town, and making contact with other 'expatriates'. Now that he knew D. was involved in the team, he was all the more eager, it was like a family affair. Sticks had a lot of respect for D., who had also been one of his role models while growing up.

'Hear wha' happ'n: Blue come check me tonight.'

D. related the encounter. Charlie listened, rubbing the back of his neck, thoughtfully. So the Spicers had made their move at last. That meant it wouldn't be long before they tried some kind of action against D. It might not be a direct hit, as they would certainly want to recover the merchandise first. They would probably try to kidnap him, Charlie explained. He looked at D. with a mischievous smile. 'I have something for you,' he said.

Leaning forward, he slipped his hand under his seat,

bringing out a brown plastic bag. He took out a cloth-wrapped bundle from it which he handed to D. Slowly, D. unfolded the layers of material and uncovered a shiny, silver hand gun. He sat there, staring silently at the weapon.

'Browning Hi-Power 9mm automatic.' Charlie gave him an expert run down on the gun. 'Fast reload, 14-round magazine, plus one in the chamber. Medium trigger action and no jamming. I got it from one white customer of mine. Can't be traced. The numbers have been burned out.'

D. examined the gun carefully. It looked clean, almost new. He tried the loading mechanism, tested the trigger, firmly adjusting the butt in his hand. This was the best gun he had ever had, a long way from what he usually used back home.

'This one is for you, star,' Charlie said, handing him two magazines. 'I have a piece already.'

D. looked at his friend, moved by the gesture. 'Respect, me breddah,' he said simply.

'Cool, man,' Charlie smiled. 'Let's go to my place, we've got things to take care of.'

'Hold on, I want to check one girl I did deh wid ina de dance,' said D.

'Let Mickey go,' Charlie suggested.

D. described Jenny to the youth and let him out of the car.

'It looks like you're hungry,' Charlie said, winking at his partner.

'You know how it go,' D. retorted with a grin. 'Run-nins have to run . . .'

The two men laughed heartily. Charlie turned on the car stereo and they sat there, exchanging women stories and jokes, waiting for Sticks to return.

D. felt more relaxed now that things were happening.

41

He always preferred an outright state of war to undefined situations when both sides simply watched each other. At least now he knew what to expect. They had made their approach to him, he had refused to negotiate. Not only that, but they would soon find out that he was using their stuff to set up business with Charlie and take over some of their action. He had now added insult to injury; they would have to strike soon, and strike hard. Besides getting rid of him, they needed to put out a warning to all: no one could rip off the Spicers and get away with it.

The flame of the lighter flickered twice before it caught. Slowly, a chubby hand lifted it and placed it against the end of the glass tube. The small piece of crystal-like white fragment inside the tube ignited. Drawing sharply at the other end of the pipe, Robbie inhaled the thick smoke from the now red-hot rock. He blew out and immediately started pulling on the pipe again with a hissing sound. As he was refilling his lungs with the potent smoke, he felt the familiar rush of heat within his body and a sensation, like a jackpot being hit, at the back of his skull. Eyes closed, Robbie passed the glass tube to Sticks before leaning back in the chair. He remained there, motionless with his head tilted back and his right hand still half-outstretched.

Robbie and Sticks had already been through three pipes since arriving at Donna's house with D. two hours earlier. They were now sprawled all over the seats, too high on the potent crack mixture to speak. Sitting across from them, D. was busy checking the rolls of banknotes that covered the coffee table. He had smoked a pipe with his soldiers earlier on. His face was set and his eyes barely visible but he kept on counting the £20 and £50 notes over and over. Once he was satisfied with a bundle, he placed it in an already bulging brown leather pouch. The acrid smell of crack enveloped the living room, clouds of whitish smoke swirling around the heads of the three men before drifting slowly out through the opened window.

D. had been in England barely three months and already, following Charlie's ingenious plan, money was passing through his hands as if he was printing it himself. The cocaine he had brought over had been processed in the 'labs' they had set up, and all the wash-rock produced from it sold within three weeks. At great profit. D. had reinvested most of the money in another buy which Charlie had arranged through his contacts in the US. Their production and retailing operation was now well established, business was booming, and everyone in their team was earning nicely.

As a prosperous businessman, D. had invested in his image and bought himself an almost new green Mercedes coupe. Several tailor-made suits, silk shirts, trousers, and expensive soft-leather shoes completed his style and made him one of the sharpest dressers in town. As a final and compulsory touch, he had completed his look with an extensive range of expensive gold jewellery. For a newly arrived 'immigrant', he looked like a million dollars. Understandably, he had become an instant celebrity in his new area, as much for his style as for his seemingly endless supply of crack. He had acquired a considerable following amongst the ghetto youths, eager to work for this new *don* and reap rich rewards.

Charlie was content with handling the supply side of the operation, regularly arranging for new consignments and ensuring that his couriers were operative. He didn't mind letting D. handle the local 'public relations' and supervise the security aspect of things. On the whole, they complemented each other well.

Whenever Charlie and D. appeared together at dances or shows, surrounded by their crew, they enjoyed the respect of the crowds. To add to his new fame, stories of D.'s past deeds back in Jamaica began to circulate around town, boosting his image even more. Having left Kingston where he was a name to be reckoned with, D. enjoyed his new popularity and made the most of it. He could walk into almost any club or venue without paying, and people were always buying him drinks, eager to be counted amongst his friends. His life now was the way he had always thought it should be, and he intended for it to go on that way.

Absorbed as he was in his accounts, D. had not heard the door open. Suddenly aware of being watched, he looked up and was surprised to see Donna standing over him. By the look on her face, she was upset. He greeted her but didn't get any answer. Robbie and Sticks were too far gone to notice anything much, staring blankly at a cartoon on the TV.

'Me and you have to talk, D.' Donna's voice was cold. She turned around and walked out of the room.

D. sat there for a while, wondering whether to start recounting the wad of notes in his hand, or to find out what upset Donna. He decided for the latter and got up. He found Donna in the bedroom, staring out of the window.

'Is what happen, baby,' D. asked pleasantly.

Donna stood still for a while longer, then slowly turned to face him. Her eyes were still and slightly veiled in a way that caused D. to drop his innocent smile. 'Tell me something, D.; you remember I tell you seh I don't want none a dem t'ings in yah?!' Donna sounded very serious.

D. tried to cool her down. 'Ah true, is just t'rough dem youth did smoke earlier on, but I will make sure it don't happen again.'

'Dat is only one t'ing. I try fe raise up a child in yah, and you know, man, and I don't want to see her around

45

drugs and guns.' Donna continued to air her grievances. 'Yeah, you gwan raise your eyebrows; you t'ink I don't know seh you keep gun in yah?! Well, I tell you before; I can't stop you from dealing with dem t'ings, but I don't want not'ing to do with it.'

Donna turned back towards the window, her face contracted by anger. In a softer tone she said, 'Unless you stop bringing your business ina de house, I don't really want you in yah.'

Leaning against the door, D. listened to the rebuke, knowing she must have kept her feelings inside for a long time.

'You don't have to get vex, Donna, man. Business working nice, you can have anyt'ing you want, you know.' He tried to sound smooth.

Donna turned back towards him and shook her head. She sighed. 'You're not hearing what I'm saying, D. Money don't mean that much to me, I have been doing al'right up to now.'

'Doing al'right?' D. smirked. 'You doing al'right, yes, but you have to get up at six every morning and do two jobs to earn enough. You can live better than that Donna, and without slaving.'

'Oh, so you want me to sell drugs too for a living? Let me tell you somet'ing; is plenty man me see come from Yard and believe seh dem ah go make it big dem way deh. You know what happen to them, eh?' Donna was intent on speaking her mind now. 'Well, dem is either in jail, or get deported, some even end up dead. Is dem kind a life you come look yah?'

D. felt the argument had gone too far. He kissed his teeth and tried to walk away, but Donna went on: 'You know what will happen when police come raid this house? Dem will take me down to jail, same way like you. You believe seh you too smart for dem English police? Make me tell you, don't take dem simple, just though dem nah carry gun don't mean not'ing. Dem will mash up your life. No sah, I don't want not'ing to do with drugs, and if you ah deal with dat, stay away from me. Furthermore, I don't need any money from dat . . .'

D. decided that he had heard enough. Donna was determined to upset him. It was better to leave before he lost his temper.

'Al'right,' he shouted while walking away, 'you t'ink seh I need to stay in dis house? I have better places to go to, you watch me . . .'

D. marched into the living room, a frown on his face. Sticks and Robbie were emerging from their lethargic state.

'Mek we laf yah, y'hear sah.'

Sensing anger in D.'s voice, the two youths promptly got up and gathered their stuff. Quickly, D. put the money left on the table inside the leather bag and they marched out of the flat.

'Wha happ'n to my curry-goat, skipper?'

Robbie was getting impatient. He had ordered the food fifteen minutes before and was still waiting. The small café was now almost full with hungry customers, all trying to get served first and shouting their orders at the bearded man and his helper behind the counter. At that hour of the day, around one o'clock, there was always a noisy crowd inside G.B.'s, taking in the music while waiting for their meals. Situated on the 'front line', the main street where all the wheeling and dealing happened in this area of East London, the restaurant catered for the tastes of most of the community. Jamaican-born youths especially, most of them being particular about their food, enjoyed G.B.'s cooking, which was the nearest they could get to the authentic Caribbean flavour.

While waiting for his meal, Robbie was talking to a girl he had seen on the street several times before. Today, as she passed the café, he had called out to her and convinced her to stop and talk to him. The girl explained that she was on her way to college, but the persistent Robbie had cajoled her into coming inside for a few minutes. He could see that the girl was shy and uncomfortable amongst the mainly Yardie crowd. They were standing near the entrance, Robbie whispering in her ear that he saw her walk past regularly and thought she was the prettiest girl in the area. Sensitive to the compliment, the girl smiled and, looking at her watch, insisted that she had to go or would be late for her class. Robbie put on his most innocent and tender look and told her that he understood but would really like to meet her later. He could see that he had succeeded in breaking through the girl's initial reluctance, he just needed more time with her. He finally managed to get a promise from the girl, whose name was Karen, to meet him at the same spot after college. He watched her hurry away, feeling quite satisfied with himself.

'You nah want the curry-goat again, Big Youth,' G.B. shouted from behind the counter. He had taken the habit of calling Robbie by that nickname, with reference to his large frame.

'How you mean!' replied Robbie, making his way to the front.

He paid for the food and decided against eating it in the café. Walking out, he headed towards the nearby Cromwell pub where he had left Sticks playing pool. The sun was shining, yet a cool October breeze announced the coming winter. England was fine, except for the cold months which made everything look grey and miserable.

It would be Robbie's second winter in London, and he didn't look forward to it, but he thought of this inconvenience as a minor price to pay for a better life.

He was about to cross the street towards the pub when he noticed the dark red Volvo which had been driving behind him at slow speed since he left the restaurant. Glancing briefly to his right, he saw the vehicle stop. He tried in vain to see the driver through the smoked-glass windscreen. As he reached the opposite side of the road, he heard a sudden screech of tyres and the roar of the big engine coming in his direction. He spun around.

The Volvo was heading straight towards him. His brain went blank . . .

The big car came to a sudden halt less than five yards from him. His back against the iron railings of a gate, he saw the passenger and rear doors fly open as two men came out. He didn't recognize the faces but saw the ugly muzzle of a large gun in the hand of one of the men. Realizing he had nowhere to run, Robbie dropped the paper bag he was holding and stood still, his mind empty. The gunman was standing a yard away from him now. He was about the same age as Robbie and wore a heavy leather jacket and a furry black Kangol hat. He held the gun low, directed towards Robbie's stomach. The other man was darker than his accomplice, tall and slim with a face without expression. Calmly, he walked up to the frozen Robbie and stared at him.

'Where you ah go so fast, *bwoy*?' The tall man had stressed the last word, giving it all the insulting connotation it carried in Jamaican talk.

'Is what ouno want?' Robbie asked, trying to keep his composure.

'Gimme your drugs, man,' the man said in a cold voice.

49

Robbie's mind was ticking fast. He started to figure it out; the two men had to be working for the Spicers. No one else in their right mind would rob their outfit. He asked, 'Star, you know who me ah work for?'

The youth with the gun hadn't moved. The tall man seemed to be in charge of the operation.

'Yes, bwoy, and you can tell your boss that we gwan close ouno down,' the man replied with a wicked grin while he held out his hand.

Robbie knew it was pointless trying anything. Even if he managed to reach for the knife in his back pocket, he wouldn't have much of a chance. He felt a cold anger gripping his guts. Closely watched by the soldier with the big gun, he took out the pouch from his jacket. Inside, there were about a dozen small plastic bags each containing a piece of white rock. The man with the stone face took it from him. Then, reading the anger on Robbie's face, he smirked, 'This is your lucky day, *bwoy*, next time you must pick up a corn.'

He signalled to his soldier and the two men climbed back in the car which drove away at speed. Robbie stood on the pavement for a short while, controlling his fury. Maybe he should feel lucky. The Spicers usually made a point of shooting their victims. He had no doubt that they were behind the attack, who else would rob one of D.'s team in broad daylight, on the front line?! Although his outfit was the target, Robbie took the incident personally. Business had to be taken care of first, but he would make a point of avenging himself of the insult. A frown on his face, he picked up his food and hurried towards the pub.

The music from the stereo was loud enough for a party. On the television screen, scenes from a movie silently unfolded. Lying on the sofa, a glass of orange juice in one hand and the TV remote control in the other, D. digested the breakfast he had just finished eating. He kept switching from channel to channel, mechanically, while taking in the lyrics of the sound system cassette he had been given the previous evening. Recordings of sessions of the best Jamaican sounds were prized items for those exiled in England like D. True, there were good UK-based sounds, and the leading sets from Jamaica usually came over on tour several times a year. Yet, the feel was nothing compared to Yard sound clashes, when two, or even three, sounds 'stringed-up' on a lawn in the electric atmosphere of the Jamaican night. Listening to a cassette of one of these dances, D. could close his eyes and almost be there. It was his link to his roots.

Besides entertaining, sound systems also fulfilled another important function in Jamaica; they were by and large the only news medium available to the masses. In a country where newspapers were relatively too expensive for most of the population and where, until recently, illiteracy still existed to an extent, sound systems kept everyone informed of the latest developments both on the national and international scene. The most trivial events of Jamaica's domestic life, in particular those that could be interpreted with humour, provided the various sound system DJs with ready-made material. Similarly, international politics and world affairs could be shaped into lyrics by the ever inventive Jamaican youths. For the previous generation, those of D.'s age group, lyrics from the sound systems had been the staple diet during their school days. At that time, the Rasta movement was the dominant influence in the life of the island and every song that came out of the leading studios of the era expounded on the Bible, African history, or Black consciousness. But

51

times had changed; the lyrics coming from D.'s cassette were rooted in much more basic topics. The connection to the present state of the ghetto social, or rather anti-social, life, the violence and the drugs, wasn't hard to make. DJs, or MCs as they preferred to be known, such as Shabba Ranks, Supercat, Ninjaman, and Cobra now carried the swing and the substance of their lyrics had fast become the dogmas all dancehall ravers lived by.

D. stretched lazily and got up to play the other side of the cassette. He had come home late the night before, after spending some time gambling and raving at Shortie's, a local after-hours illegal drinking den. He usually got up about noon and didn't start his moves until about four in the afternoon, especially now that the weather had turned rather cold. Most of the time, he was too deep in his sleep to notice when Jenny left for work, early in the morning. D. had moved in with her shortly after leaving Donna's house. By that time, he had been seeing Jenny regularly for a few months. She had been happy to have him move in with her and, after a few adjustments due mostly to his ways, things were going fine.

With the music back on, D. sat in the sofa and took the spliff he had left in the ashtray earlier on. After breakfast, he usually rolled up a mix of tobacco, ganja, and a sprinkle of cocaine, as a kind of boost to start his day. Back in Jamaica he had been exposed to drugs early, through the people he worked for, but had never got involved with it. However, since arriving in England, his way of life had changed in this respect.

D. lit the spliff. He leaned back, listening to the music and smoking. Looking at his watch he was surprised to see it was only just past one o'clock. He didn't feel like staying in to watch videos as he often did in the afternoon. He reached over for the phone affixed to the wall near the sofa and dialled Charlie's mobile number. The line was busy. Charlie had insisted that they should carry cell phones to keep in touch at all times. Also, these types were difficult to tap, so it was possible to discuss certain details more freely than on home phones. D. decided to drive to Hackney, he would surely find someone from their team on the line. He glanced through the window at the grey sky and went for his thick chequered jumper in the bedroom. On his way back, he grabbed his grey Trilby hat on the coat hanger and stopped by the mirror to adjust it. Satisfied with his look, he switched off the stereo and the TV, slipped a wad of notes in his back pocket, took his keys, and headed for the door.

Outside the flats, he turned right to reach the parking lot at the back. He unlocked his car and got in. He liked the Mercedes. For years he had watched with envy as the big shots drove up and down Spanish Town Road in their gleaming imported cars. He always knew that one day he too would be gliding in one. Now every day, as he drove around London, he smiled to himself for having made that dream come true. Smoothly, he backed the sports car out of the parking bay and went around the block, taking the slope leading to the High Street. Highbury was a nice area, more upmarket than Hackney where he did business. D. felt good about living far from the hustling scene. Very few people knew where he lived, and only Charlie ever came to visit him there. Casually steering the wheel with one hand, he drove down the Holloway Road at good speed, rocked by the music from the large speakers behind him.

On reaching the area, D. decided to make a stop at Leroy's record shop. Although they were not involved in the same business, Leroy and D. kept in close contact. D. loved to spend time at the shop, checking the latest releases and talking to acquaintances. At times, he would use the back room to negotiate a deal with someone, but Leroy insisted that no actual trading should take place on his premises. That was cool with D. He respected Leroy and understood his concern for the business. His record shop was sometimes full of characters who bore little love for each other, and only needed an opportunity to settle past disputes, but no arguments ever took place there. The place was effectively neutral ground. Leroy saw to that.

As he parked the car on the opposite side of the road, D. noticed a boy astride a bicycle in front of the shop, looking at him. He had seen him around several times before. The boy, whose name was Harry, was always offering to wash his car or run errands for him. He couldn't be more than twelve but was streetwise and bold. Harry had told D. that his mother had taken him to Jamaica on holidays the year before, and that he was *rough*. He stayed away from school whenever he could, thriving on hanging around places where kids his age shouldn't be.

D. crossed the road and stopped in front of Harry. 'Whapp'n, youth?'

'Al'right, D.' The boy's face was serious.

'So you don't go to school today?' D. enquired.

'I got suspended.' Harry sounded proud.

D. looked at him with a frown. 'Suspended? What dem suspend you for?'

'They said I hit the teacher,' Harry answered.

D. raised his eyebrows. Even he had never done anything like that. Looking straight in the boy's face, he asked, 'So wha', you hit him fe true?'

'I had an argument with a boy and the teacher grabbed me by my collar, so I kicked him,' Harry said, shrugging.

D. couldn't help laughing. He couldn't really blame the boy for his reaction. Harry was definitely *rough*.

'What your mother said?' D. asked.

Harry sighed. 'She said I cause her too much problems. She told me to go and stay with my father.'

'Where your father live?' D. enquired, curious to find out more about the young renegade.

'He lives in Stamford Hill, but his woman don't like me.'

Harry didn't seem worried by the situation. He spoke with the resigned tone of a grown man who just had a stroke of bad luck. Like many boys his age, he had grown too fast, in an environment where childhood is but a brief moment. D. shook his head. He took a five-pound note out of his pocket and handed it to Harry.

'Hear wha': go down G.B.'s and get me some carrot juice. You can use the rest of the money for yourself, seen?!'

Harry took the money, flashed a toothy grin, and sped away on his bike. D. watched him disappear in the traffic, before walking inside the shop. There were only five customers, one of them involved in a lively discussion with Leroy. D. stepped up to the counter and nodded to Leroy. The big man smiled back at him. The latest hot favourite was spinning on the turntable, the bass bouncing deafeningly about the walls of the small room. D. leaned against the counter, absorbing the pulse of the rhythm.

After listening to a few records and seeing that Leroy was still busy, D. walked to the end of the counter and turned left into the small back room. Only a few of Leroy's friends were allowed there. As D. pushed the door open, the strong aroma of ganja assaulted his nostrils. At the other end of the room, a cloud of smoke enveloped a figure sitting in a chair. Piper was looking at D. through the haze.

'Hail, me lion!' The voice was a deep baritone, like a ship's horn.

'Iree, Jahman.' D. smiled at the elder Dread.

Piper was well known around town. He was old enough to be D.'s father. He had been in England for years. He often spent time in the back room, where he could listen to music while smoking and meditating. Piper had worked in the community for a long time, setting up projects to train young people in various crafts, teaching drumming and coaching football teams. He was loved and respected by all in the community as a man of deep faith and education. It was said that he had graduated from university many years before, and that his boundless knowledge extended to numerous disciplines. Piper had witnessed the development of the black community over the last twenty years, being one of the first Dreads to come to England. He knew Leroy's family back in Jamaica and remembered him as a little boy. It was Piper's influence that helped Leroy to change his ways and settle down when he came over. They were like father and son.

D. sat on a bench across from the older man. Piper's face was like weathered parchment, the lines on his dark, shiny skin cutting shallow grooves that told the story of his journey. He had a soft, illuminating smile but his eyes were deep and piercing, like bolts of black steel. With long, thick, and greying locks framing his features, he looked like a figure from the Old Testament.

'Build a spliff, man.' Piper slowly leaned forward and handed D. a small plastic bag half full with dark green herb.

D. thanked him. He took some paper out of his pocket and proceeded to roll a joint. Piper lit up his smoke, then passed him the matches. D. could feel the Dread's eyes upon him through the white clouds. They smoked in silence for a while, except for the sound of music filtering through the door.

'I hear seh one boy get shot outside Rocco's couple days ago,' Piper said finally.

D. drew on his spliff. He had heard about the incident from one of his soldiers who was at the scene that night. 'Yeah, I hear 'bout dat.' D. nodded. 'Some youths get in a argument about one girl, one left the place and come back with a matic. Shot one boy ina de head, twice.'

Piper tapped his spliff lightly, dropping the ashes on the floor. He drew deeply, then blew out the smoke before saying, 'Too many youths dead fe not'ing.' He looked at D. 'Is like dem cyan wait fe kill someone. Any lickle t'ing, dem lick shot.'

D. could feel the strength of the herb boosting his high some more. His mind was tuned in to the Dread's line of thought. Yet he was weary of getting too involved in this particular topic.

'T'ings rough out deh, you know, Rasta,' he said softly.

'True, t'ings rough, dat is why me cry fe see the way we ah kill one another.'

Piper had a grave look on his face. He continued. 'One time, if two man have a quarrel dem would fight it out with dem strength. At the worst, one would get cut up but not'ing more. Nowadays, it's pure killing. And fe wha'? Vanity; gold, money, drugs, even woman. Truly, man worse than beast.'

The Dread shook his head sadly. D. didn't say anything. He knew Piper was right. He heard the door open and turned his head. Harry walked up to him, holding a paper bag.

'Iree, Dread,' he greeted Piper.

'Iree, youthman.' Piper looked at the boy thoughtfully.

D. took the bag Harry handed to him. He asked, 'You get some food for yourself?'

'Yeah, I eat it already.' Harry nodded.

'Al'right, you go check your mother later on.' The boy frowned as D. spoke.

'Look now, you don't have no quarrel with your mother, she just worry about you. Go home and talk to her, seen?!'

Harry sighed and said, 'OK, I'll go meet her after work.'

'Nice. Hit me, star!'

D. held out a closed fist, Harry touched it with his, in the way youths greeted each other in the ghetto.

Repressing a proud smile, Harry held out a fist to Piper, who touched it in the same manner. The boy turned and left the two men.

The sound of music filled the room then decreased in volume again as the door opened and closed. D. took the container out of the bag and took a sip of the carrot juice after offering some to Piper who refused politely. The Dread gave him a penetrating look. 'Some good advice you give dat youthman,' he said.

D. grinned. He lit up his spliff again. 'Dat bwoy is al'right. Him just have some problem at school and him mother get distressed over dat.'

Piper smiled. 'You must see most ah dem youth; not'ing wrong with dem originally, but society spoil dem.' The Dread waited a few seconds, carefully selecting his words. He went on.

'Me seh society spoil dem, because it show dem dat money is all dat matters. Yet at the same time, education is set up a way dat mek dem feel it is of no value to dem. Imagine, a youth see a man who have a criss car, jewellery, and nice clothes and him know seh is not work and education the man get it t'rough. You nah feel seh the youth will want to do the same t'ing dat man do fe get money?'

Piper left the question hanging in the air. D. knew he wasn't really expected to answer. He knew exactly what Piper was talking about.

'Is truth you ah talk, Jahman,' D. said after a while. 'Black people cyan get a break in dis time unless it's t'rough music or sports. If a man don't have dem form of skills, him still ha fe make a living differently. Dat is why we must take some risks, try fe de best.'

Piper was leaning back in the chair now, looking into D.'s eyes in a curious way. D. almost felt as if the Dread could read his thoughts as they formed in his mind. He lit the rest of his spliff and said, 'The fittest shall survive, dat is what the Bible seh.'

'What good is it if a man gain the whole world and lose his own soul,' Piper added, also quoting the Scriptures.

D. smiled, thoughtfully. As he was reflecting on Piper's answer, the door opened and Leroy called out: 'D., someone on the phone for you.'

D. got up and walked towards the door. Before leaving the room, he looked at the elder Rastaman and nodded; there was something about the Dread he couldn't quite define, a sense of timelessness about him. But worldly cares were calling him, breaking Piper's spell. He took the phone, listened to Robbie's report, then left the shop in a hurry.

t was only a game of dominoes, but to an outside observer it might have seemed as if an ugly fight was about to break out. The four men around the table had their eyes riveted on the line of small black rectangles. Amidst suspicious looks, curses, and exhortations, each man in turn slammed his play on the board with shattering force, derisively taunting the next player to follow his move. The atmosphere was tense. The few observers surrounding the game wisely refrained from any comment that might appear to cast doubt on any of the players' skill. These were regular contestants in the challenges that took place more or less every night at Shortie's. Black Jack and dices were being played at other tables, but the domino game was always the noisiest. Several times before, after a particularly disputed game, opponents had to be restrained and warned by the bouncers who took care of the security of the place.

'Card!' Kelly announced, his closed hand held high above his head.

Straight-faced, D. checked the two pieces he had left. Winston's eyes were switching from the two dominoes in his hand to the last play on the table. D. knew that no matter what Winston played, he was the one who would make or break the game. He and Kelly had already won two of the three games that night. If they won this one too, they would win the contest. Across the table from Winston, his partner Longers was getting impatient. If they managed to win, it would be a draw and the two teams would have to play a decisive game for the £100 stake. For now, Winston had difficulties making up his mind: he was desperately trying to guess which two pieces D. still had in his hand.

'Cho, is wha' you a do, man? Play weh me want nuh!' Longers' face reflected the almost palpable tension around the table.

With a last furtive look towards D., Winston slammed down his card on the board. There was total silence for a few seconds. D. leaned back in his chair. Longers sighed heavily. Across from D., Kelly was still clinching his remaining domino, a cigarette hanging from the corner of his mouth. Winston looked in turn at the game, then at Longers, then at D.

'Well, Longers, it looks like the game is up to me now,' D. said with a grin.

Longers didn't answer. His jaws were clenched tight, his eyes lowered on the single domino in his crooked right hand. He knew that if D. made the wrong play, the game was his. Alternatively, he might have to concede his second consecutive defeat to D. and Kelly this week, and pay them again. Longers didn't like losing. He was known to have a bad temper and many simply preferred to stay away from a challenge with him, rather than risk provoking the tall and bony man's wrath.

D. was enjoying every minute of suspense; he took a sip from the beer bottle in front of him, scratched his head then looked around the table at the intense faces of the three other players. He glanced at the two pieces in his hand for the last time, picked up one and held it high.

'Al'right, if I wrong we lose,' he said teasingly.

With a deafening crack, his hand crashed on to the table. Three pairs of eyes followed the move, remaining fixed on the domino that now ended the long twisted line.

There was silence again. Kelly was looking at Longers now. Both Winston and Longers were staring at the play. D. took another sip from his beer, seemingly unconcerned. He felt confident that Longers couldn't finish the play with his piece.

'Your play . . .' Longers finally said in a low voice, without looking at Kelly. He was frowning.

Kelly tossed his last domino indifferently on to the table. The game was over.

'We win again,' D. said stretching himself.

Longers said nothing. He knew he had been beaten fairly but felt angry all the same. It wasn't so much the money. He could afford to lose that amount without worrying about it. Rather, it was a matter of pride. In the ghetto, where they had all grown up, reputation was everything and even a simple game of dominoes could prove to be an embarrassment for a man such as Longers. He got up.

'We can give ouno another chance tomorrow,' D. said, seemingly accommodating. In fact, that made the losers feel even more frustrated. D. knew about Longers' temper, but he couldn't help teasing. Besides, he was confident that the lanky man wasn't crazy enough to try and test him. He watched closely as Longers put his hand to his back pocket, just in case.

'See the money here.' The unhappy loser grudgingly dropped £50 on the table and walked off towards the other room. He hadn't looked at Winston since the last play.

Winston paid his dues and departed also. Kelly shared the money. He smiled as he handed D. the crumpled banknotes.

'You frightened me for a while, star.'

'I follow the play from early, dem couldn't fool me,' D. laughed.

He and Kelly were often domino partners at Shortie's.

Kelly was a broad, brown-skinned man with a nice smile. He wore a diamond stud in his left ear and several heavy gold rings on both hands. He had recently been released from prison after serving almost two of a three-year sentence for drugs offences. As he had explained to D., it was all a misunderstanding.

Kelly's main line of work was keeping the string of girls who worked the beat for him happy. He didn't really deal in drugs. He made a living from the girls' earnings and also supplied them with cocaine and crack. As most hookers used drugs to withstand the rigour of their trade, Kelly was making good. It was while he was on his way to bring some stuff over to one of the girls' places that he had been stopped by a squad car for a traffic offence. An over-zealous officer had decided to search the car, and as a result Kelly soon found himself spending a 'vacation' in Brixton prison for the next few years. With a lenient judge and a good lawyer, he would have gotten away with a lighter sentence, if it hadn't been for the untimely reminder by the prosecution of an assault conviction some years before.

D. bought two beers at the bar and the two men stepped into the smaller dark and smoky room, mingling with the crowd of dancers. They stayed there for the next hour, smoking and talking, until D. decided to take his leave. Jenny had once again complained that she never saw him, and that he never spent the evening with her, so a few days ago he had promised to stay home. He hadn't managed it so far this week. As it was now past two o'clock, she would be sleeping. He had meant to get home early, but the incident with Robbie had changed his plans.

D. had spent most of the afternoon at Charlie's house discussing what their response should be. The Spicers had finally moved against him, though it was a surprisingly

63

low-key step. From Robbie's description of his assailants, D. had recognized Blue. The action sounded more like a warning, and that wasn't usual procedure. After an animated debate, D. had decided to increase the security around their operation and told Sticks to recruit a surveillance team to keep tag on any move by all known Spicers soldiers. Robbie was all for avenging the assault immediately but, D. explained, there was more at stake than personal honour. Besides, the action was directed at him, Robbie was only targeted because he was one of his soldiers. Just in case, Charlie had asked Indian, his top lieutenant, to have some weapons ready. If war couldn't be avoided they had to be ready.

Kelly was busy dancing with a girl. D. waved to him and stepped out of the room. On his way to the stairs, he was stopped by Tina, one of Charlie's girlfriends. She asked him if he had 'anything', as she couldn't find Charlie and needed some rock. He lied that he didn't know where his friend was and that he couldn't help her. He knew Charlie was keeping away from her because she was a junkie. Tina was one of a number of girls in the area who were constantly looking for drugs. As they couldn't afford to buy the amount of crack they needed each day, and no man was prepared to support them, they turned to offering their services for money or crack. They were prepared to do anything for a piece of rock. D. had no time for her. He left her there, begging, and left the joint.

The air outside was cold. This was the first winter D. had to face and he feared what it would be like in a few months' time. He walked up the dark alley towards the main street where his car was parked, his hands in his pockets. As he turned right into the street, a chilly wind slapped his face and he fixed his hat.

The Mercedes was parked on the left about thirty

yards away. As he was about to cross the road, one of two minicab drivers leaning against their vehicles called unto him, asking if he needed a cab. There were usually a few drivers hanging around outside Shortie's at this time of night, waiting for customers. As he dismissed the offer with a wave, he noticed a car parked on the opposite side of the road, engine running. He started to cross the road. Something – a fleeting sensation in the back of his head – forced him to look at the car once more. By now he was in the middle of the empty two-way street. It was a dark Volvo. All at the same time, he remembered Robbie's story, noticed the half-opened rear window, and saw the car move forward. He was only two steps from the kerb when he heard the two distinct but mingled sounds – the roar of the powerful engine and the sharp crack of automatic gunfire.

As the car roared towards him, D. instinctively bent forward as he made for the low wall of the front garden of the house a few feet away. He leapt out of the road on to the pavement, losing his hat as he did so. The Volvo was almost level with him now. The gunfire subsided for a couple of seconds but started again close behind him. Too close. He heard a bullet whistle past his left ear. As he dived over the low wall, he felt a burning in his left arm. Even as he hit the dirt on the other side of the wall, he heard bullets scraping the cement above his head, and then the roar of the car as it sped past him.

He was over the initial surprise of the attack now. He quickly cleared his mind. They knew they had missed and would surely turn and come back to finish the job. Oblivious to the needling sensation in his arm, he crawled alongside the wall, keeping his head down, until he reached the corner, where the garden of the next house began. He went for his gun, still tucked in his belt behind

65

his back, and loaded it. Cautiously, listening for any sounds, D. ventured a look above the edge of the wall. The Volvo was parked near two phone booths, across from the small dome-shaped lawn that formed a roundabout. He couldn't see through the tinted glass, but the rear window was still opened.

D. took a sharp gulp of the cold night air and tensed himself. They had the advantage while he waited. His best chance was to attack. Although his assailants had superior fire power, he had fifteen bullets and intended to let them know about it. The lawn with the phones was fifty yards away, straight ahead. His car was only half that distance, to the left. He counted to three and jumped over the wall. Crouching low, he sprinted to the roundabout and landed flat in the grass just as the car started to move. Holding the Browning automatic with both hands, he aimed at the front window and started to fire. The windscreen shattered. From his position, he could see a man steering furiously to drive out of range of his fire. Clearly his assailants hadn't expected D. to take the initiative; the hunters were being hunted. He saw the black muzzle of a sub-machine-gun appear out of the rear window as the car passed his position, and quickly rolled to his left as bullets dug into the grass around him. He rose to his knees and fired three more shots, one of which cracked the rear window of the big car, as it sped away towards the crossroad. He thought of giving chase, but decided against it; he had been lucky enough for one night.

The night was once again silent. Only a few minutes had passed since D. had left Shortie's. As he stood there in the grass, the gun still warm in his hand, he felt a cold fury rise within him. If it hadn't been for the cab driver calling him, he might well be lying in the road, dead. It seemed like the old *science* that had saved him many times in the past was still working.

There was no time to waste, he had to leave the area before the police showed up. He slipped the gun inside his waist and started towards his car. He noticed his hat lying in the middle of the road and went to pick it up. As he brushed it with a hand, he saw the neat hole in the brim, big enough to push his finger through it. The first bullet had missed his head by inches . . . This time it was war.

D. got in the car. As he steered to drive out, he once again felt the burning sensation in his left arm. Until now, he had all but forgotten that he got hit. He felt a sticky substance soaking the inside of his jumper sleeve, near the biceps. He could still move his arm; that meant that the bullet had missed the bone. He put off seeing to the wound until later. Right now, there was business to attend to.

Steering the car with one hand, he drove at speed through the empty streets. He drove towards Homerton where Charlie had recently moved in with Charmaine, a girl who had just given him a baby boy. D. had only been there once in the daytime, but he knew he could find the house again. He recognized the turn from the main street and passed the row of houses slowly, looking for a window with fern-like plants hanging from it. He left the car in a vacant space a little further down and walked back to the house. It was late in the night but Charlie was probably still up. He usually parked at the back, out of sight from inquisitive neighbours.

D. rang the bell twice. A few seconds passed then the curtains of the first-floor window moved and a pair of eyes peered into the darkness below. There was the sound of feet on the stairs then the door opened on a smiling Charmaine.

'Hi, D.' She sounded surprised to see him. 'Come in, Charlie's upstairs.'

She closed the door behind him as he climbed to the first floor. Charlie was just coming down from the upstairs bedroom, dressed in pyjama bottoms and a sweater.

'Wait, what's happening, star?' Charlie smiled. Then he noticed the steely look on his friend's face. He frowned.

'Dem try fe dus' me outside Shortie's . . .' D. said sternly.

He showed Charlie the hole in his hat and pointed to his left arm. The blood on the jumper sleeve looked black against the thick grey wool. Charmaine, who stood silently against the staircase, put one hand on her mouth. Charlie sighed.

'Sit down, man. Let's take care of that first,' he said.

'I want to hit dem now!' D. replied in a cold voice.

'OK, I'll make some calls, it won't take long.' Charlie picked up his mobile phone and started dialling. 'Take off that jumper,' he said, waiting for the line.

D. put the hat down on a chair and began to take his top off. Charmaine, who had recovered from the initial shock of the news, helped him to slide the sleeve along his arm, slowly, to avoid brushing the wound. They took his shirt off carefully, as the material was sticking to his raw flesh. Charmaine managed to get him to sit on the sofa, where he looked at his arm. The side of the upper arm close to the chest was dark red against the brown hue of his skin. The wound had to be cleaned to determine the extent of the damage.

'It's just a scrape,' D. reassured Charmaine.

'Maybe, but you better tend to it; you never know what they shot you with,' Charlie remarked as he got off

68

the phone. He had gotten hold of Sticks at his girlfriend's house and told him to be at a certain spot with Robbie and two other soldiers in half an hour. He then got Indian out of bed and asked him to load several specific items of artillery into his car boot and meet Sticks at the same place. There was no time for explanations.

Charmaine had brought some hot water in a basin from the kitchen and was trying to clean the wound the best she could. If D. felt any pain, he wasn't showing it.

'You have any fresh pepper and a lemon?' he asked Charmaine.

The girl said she'd have a look and went to the kitchen. While she was gone, D. explained to Charlie how he had almost lost his life only a short while before. Charlie shook his head. 'Maybe what people say is true, maybe you really are jinxed,' he said jokingly.

Charmaine came back with a lemon and a piece of red pepper. She and Charlie looked on as D. took out his knife, cut the pepper into small pieces, and squeezed the lemon over it. He then mixed the potion with hot water and used his kerchief to wash the wound.

'The bullet went right through. You're lucky!' Charlie remarked.

Charmaine bandaged D.'s arm as he put on one of Charlie's sweaters.

'I'll get changed then we go,' Charlie said, starting up the stairs.

'Wait!' D. called out. 'I feel seh you shouldn't get involved in dat move.'

'What d'you mean, man?' Charlie sounded surprised at the remark.

D. looked at Charmaine, then at Charlie. Aware that she wasn't supposed to hear the conversation, she made her way to the bedroom.

'Dis is between I and dem, star. So far, dem don't want not'ing with you,' D. continued.

Charlie shook his head in disagreement. 'Look, man, we're in business together, right? That means your enemies are my enemies.'

'Dat hit wasn't business, Charlie; it was personal. I used to work for dem, remember?'

'OK, they hit you because you took from them, sure. But they want us out of the game too.' Charlie paused and looked at his friend. 'Suppose they get rid of you, do you think they will leave me alone after that? I know they've been wanting to hit me for some time.'

D. looked disturbed at the idea of Charlie taking part in the raid.

'Come on man, let's go.' Charlie was determined. 'Al'right, they won't see me. I'll stay outside and cover you,' he offered.

'OK, come on.' D. nodded.

Within ten minutes, they were in Charlie's car, driving towards the meeting point. Sticks was outside his car talking to Indian when they got there. Charlie parked his BMW and organized the convoy. He would drive in Indian's car with Indian and Robbie, D. would go with Sticks and the two other soldiers. They started out towards Harlesden, Charlie leading the way. Sticks insisted on knowing every detail of the ambush as they drove. D. wasn't in a talkative mood but told the story. At the back, Blacka and Linton, the two soldiers, were indignant at the cowardice of the shooting and full of admiration for the skill and bravery of their leader. By the time they reached Harlesden, they were prepared to kill anyone connected with those involved.

Sticks parked on the right-hand side of the road, behind Indian's car. Charlie came up to D.'s window.

'How you know the address?' D. enquired.

'I've got my sources,' Charlie replied evasively.

'So, what's the play, star?'

D. explained his plan of action. 'Dem must know the hit missed, so we have to be careful. There's a window at the back, on the garden. I take that way with Blacka and Robbie, then we can open the front door for Sticks and Linton. You and Indian keep the cars ready, just in case.'

'There could be a posse in there,' Charlie warned.

'Hear wha', I take Sticks' phone with me; anything happens outside you let me know, seen?' D. was taking no chances.

Charlie went to the boot of Indian's car and brought out a large canvas bag. He handed D. some 9mm magazines, two Uzis, and a pump-action shot-gun and some ammunition. Linton and Blacka had one 9mm handgun each. The weapons were checked and loaded, then the two cars drove up the street and parked either way from Joseph's house, on the opposite side of the road. Everyone got out as silently as possible. Indian and Charlie stayed in each car, at the ready.

The street was quiet. The five silhouettes crept silently through the gates of the house. Sticks, with one of the Uzis, and Linton took position against the main door. Meanwhile, Blacka and Robbie followed D. through the little alley which ran at the side of the house to the garden. Scenes of similar ambushes back in Jamaica flashed through D.'s mind . . .

The three men got to the back wall of the house and progressed silently to the glass garden door. Rays of light filtered through the closed curtains. D. put his ear against the glass and listened. There were at least two men in there, and some women. He signalled to Robbie who was carrying the phone to ring Charlie who in turn should alert

71

Sticks from the car that they were about to enter. D. waited for the message to get through then motioned to Blacka who was carrying a heavy sledgehammer he had taken from Sticks' car. He felt a sharp pull in his left arm as he loaded the shot-gun. Calmly, Blacka took position in front of the double glass panel, lifted the sledgehammer above his head, and, after a last look at D., sent it crashing with all his strength on the lock. There was a deafening crack as the double windows collapsed. Through the pieces of shattered wood and glass, D. stepped in, Blacka and Robbie close behind him.

Once inside, D. stepped to the middle of the room and stood there, his shot-gun firmly pointed forward. Bigga was on the sofa, a glass in his hand, too stunned to move. Joseph, who was sitting at the table in front of a small mound of white powder, tried to get up, but saw the shot-gun and sat back, very slowly. Another man was standing by the TV, very still.

Two young women, sitting beside Bigga, were staring at D., eyes wide open. While Robbie stood by D.'s side, his Uzi trained on the table, Blacka climbed the stairs to open the door for the rest of the raiding party. Sticks and Linton searched the bedrooms before coming down. No one else was in the house.

'Wait, it look like ouno having a party,' D. said with a mirthless laugh.

With his four soldiers standing in a semi-circle, their guns on Joseph and company, D. walked slowly to the table. He took off the hat he was still wearing and deftly tossed it towards Joseph.

'You should teach your boys dem to shoot straight.'

Joseph seemed puzzled. He looked at the hat with the bullet hole, then looked at D. 'If somebody shot you, it's nothing to do with me,' he said in a flat tone of voice.

D. pulled up a chair and sat opposite Joseph. He laid the shot-gun on the table, the barrel facing the short man, and leaned back in the chair. He looked around the room. Bigga hadn't moved; he visibly felt uncomfortable facing the heavily armed intruders.

'Hey! Fat bwoy, you know anyt'ing about it?' D. asked him with a scornful look.

Bigga was no coward, but he knew that unless they could convince D. of their innocence, he and Joseph were as good as dead. He tried to sound as truthful as he could.

'We not responsible for dis, star.'

D. sighed. He hadn't come here to talk. In a flash, he grabbed the shot-gun in his right hand and stuck the barrel against Joseph's throat, pressing hard. Joseph made a choking sound and raised his two arms up in surrender.

'Hold on. . . .don't shoot . . .'

The short man tried to speak, despite the cold steel crushing his larynx. His eyes were wide with fear.

'You ha fe believe we, D. The hit don't come from here, it's the truth,' he finally managed to say.

D. didn't release the pressure. 'So wha'? You soon tell me seh Blue nah work fe ouno again!' D.'s face was contorted with cold anger. His finger was tight on the trigger. Despite the pain in his throat, Joseph tried to sound convincing.

'Blue? Is Blue shot you?' Joseph had difficulties swallowing. 'I neva send him, God know . . .'

'We nah response fe Blue, star,' Bigga intervened from his corner. 'Blue report directly to the boss.'

D. squinted towards the big man. 'No lie nah go save ouno tonight.' He turned to Sticks. 'Make we dus' the whole ah dem and lef yah.'

Sticks took two steps forward. He raised the Uzi chest-high, pointing towards Bigga. One of the girls, who

73

had been huddling on the sofa in silence all the time, sobbed.

'We tell you the truth, D.' Joseph made one last try at saving their lives. 'We don't even see Blue since last week.'

D. raised his left hand, stopping Sticks. He planted his eyes into Joseph's and asked coldly, 'Is who control Blue?'

Joseph could read death in the dark eyes. He was sweating from pain and fright. 'Fox,' he said in a hoarse voice.

D. frowned. He looked towards Bigga. The big man nodded. 'We only control the supply and distribution. Fox supervises the finances and security.'

Bigga was breathing heavily.

Slowly, D. released the pressure on Joseph's throat. His mind was working fast, weighing up the information. He didn't know Fox, but had heard of him. Joseph coughed.

The third man was still standing by the TV. He hadn't moved during the whole interrogation. He was in his thirties, of medium height with a dark brown complexion and a thin moustache. Dressed in a light grey suit, he didn't seem scared. He just stood there with what looked like a glint of amusement in his slanted eyes. D. stared at him briefly.

'Who is you?' he asked.

The man waited a few seconds before answering. 'Chin,' he said simply.

His thoughts still on the business at hand, D. took a few seconds to register the name. He took a closer look at the man.

'Tony Chin?' he asked.

The man didn't reply. Smiling, he said, 'I heard about you a lot, man.'

D. was thinking fast. He lost interest in Joseph temporarily. He needed to know what Chin was doing here.

Tony Chin was something of a legend in Jamaica. He had been one of the earliest 'settlers' in Miami. During the early seventies, it became common practice for youths from the deprived West Kingston slums to slip into the United States through various means, for short 'business' trips. On arrival, a man would visit an established member of the Jamaican community in New York and, with the right recommendation, he would be given a weapon. The next step for the youth was to identify the right target for a robbery and carry it through. More often than not drug dealers, especially Latin American ones, were the ideal victims. Once his business was successfully completed, the man would return the gun to its rightful owner, with a fee, and quickly make his way back to Jamaica before his victim could trace him. Many had returned home with pockets full of US dollars and their chest adorned with 'cargo' – the thick gold chains and medallions which are the outward signs of success. Others were less lucky. Their bodies would be flown back home for burial after a wrong move in the jungle of the American ghettos.

Having made similar débuts, Chin decided not to return to his native land. He was smart and hungry and wanted to make a fresh start. So, after depriving a Puerto Rican of a quantity of cocaine, five thousand dollars, and some jewellery, the ambitious young man made his way to Miami where he contacted some old friends. Tony Chin was different from the others. He wasn't interested in robbing drugs dealers, not in the long term anyway. His dream was to establish a serious operation importing and supplying the drugs everyone wanted so much. At the time, importing was not that difficult, provided that one had reliable contacts, both in Jamaica and South America.

Within six months of arriving in Miami, Chin and the gang he had formed were smuggling an average of 50 kilos a month by air or sea. This had to be sold rapidly to cut down the risks, and in order to do so, the market had to be controlled. That was when Tony Chin became a name to be reckoned with in the state of Florida. Until then, the Cubans had been the unrivalled masters. They imported most of the cocaine that arrived in the state and, through sheer numbers, had the whole market firmly in their hands. Their only problem at that time were groups of Colombian gangsters intent on taking a share of the supplying business.

Suddenly, everything changed. Chin managed to gather enough muscle under his command and decided that the Cubans' reign was over. There ensued a bloody takeover that was to change the face of the American drug scene for ever. Being Latin, Cubans and Colombians had quite violent temperaments anyway, but their leaders knew that bloodshed was bad for business and kept it to a minimum. The Jamaicans had no such scruples.

Without warning, Tony Chin's posse started their move; dealers were robbed and sometimes shot, while customers were persuaded to buy exclusively from Chin. The resistance that the Cubans tried to put up was ruthlessly dealt with. For several months, fierce gun battles erupted all over the state, from Orlando to Palm Beach, with the worst of the violence occurring in the Black neighbourhoods. Finally, the Cubans asked to negotiate. Their chiefs met Chin and his lieutenants, and after hours of angry discussions, punctuated by violent outbursts, the two sides came to an agreement. Chin got what he wanted. He would cover all the Black ghettos and a few other areas, while the Cubans earned the right to operate in the remainder of their territory without interference. It was through this new situation that the Spicers, a loose gang formed in the back streets of Rema in the early seventies, gained a foothold in the United States.

All went well for Tony Chin until one of his henchmen got himself killed by Colombians while trying to close a deal. Chin traced and hunted down the killers. Rumour has it that he personally hacked two of the Colombians to death with a machete. The police investigated the killings, arrested Chin and some of his people, and sentenced them to seven years each. That was the last D. knew of Tony Chin, until he realized he was standing before him in Joseph's front room.

'Sit down now, man!' D. thought it wise to show some respect.

Chin walked to the chair at D.'s left, and sat down. The four soldiers, still covering the room with their weapons, realized something unexpected was happening.

D. asked, 'So, is when you come out, Don?'

'About three months now.' Chin's voice had a slight Yankee twang to it. 'Dem deport me back home after four years.'

D. turned to Joseph, who was still massaging his throat, and pointed to the cocaine spread on a magazine in front of him. Joseph pushed it towards D. who then passed the offering to Chin. The man nodded, acknowledging the mark of respect. On a sign from D., Sticks took some paper, cigarettes, and a small herb bag from his pocket and placed it all in front of Chin.

Once he and D. had built a spliff and lit up, D. asked, 'Tell me somet'ing, Don, you see Skeets ah Yard?'

Chin blew out some smoke. He looked at D. 'Yeah, him kinda vex about your move, you know.'

'I figured dat.' D. looked straight into Chin's slanted eyes and asked, 'Him order the hit?'

There was silence in the room. Tony Chin sighed. 'Skeets seh you must repay the money.'

D. wasn't satisfied with the answer but he knew that he had to take time with a man like Chin. Seeing the frustration on D.'s face, Chin tried to draw a card. 'I've been away for a long time, star. I only hear things.'

D. was too smart to buy that line. 'Hear wha'; I know I must face the consequences for what I do. I only need to know who wants me dead.' D. paused, tilted his head to the right, and grinned. 'Don, no matter weh you deh, I know dat not'ing ah gwan with the Spicers weh you nah know.'

Slowly, Chin passed his hand over his mouth. He was looking straight into D.'s eyes as he said, 'All I can tell you; I don't feel seh Skeets wants your life.'

D. stood the stare for a few seconds. Tony Chin had just made him understand, as subtly as possible, that he knew more than he could say at the present time.

Nothing more could be achieved here tonight. After asking Chin a few more questions about Miami and other business matters, D. decided to take his leave.

'Tell Blue he shouldn't have missed,' he told Joseph with a smirk.

Chin watched D. as he climbed up the stairs surrounded by his soldiers. 'Take it easy, D.,' he said.

D. saluted him. They would have to meet again.

The squad made their way out of the house. No one asked D. any questions. They could see that he was busy thinking about the encounter.

'What's happening, man? I thought you were gonna sleep in there,' Charlie said as they got to the cars.

D. looked at him thoughtfully.

'Blue wasn't there,' he said. 'But Chin was . . .'

He left Charlie with a puzzled expression on his face and got into the other car.

The little boy giggled as his mother lifted him up above her head and blew air in his face. At barely three months of age, he had already shown signs of being precocious and was the pride of his parents. Charmaine still looked at her son in amazement, as if she could hardly believe he was hers. Charlie too loved Marcus. He was the only thing that made him feel relaxed and happy after the harsh reality of the streets. Sitting back on the sofa, he smiled at the sight of mother and baby enjoying each other. Though he had a few girlfriends, Charlie felt comfortable with Charmaine and he was glad she had his child. Most women who grew up in England and America were too westernized for his taste. They tended to be inclined to jealousy, inquisitive, and argumentative. In many ways, Charmaine was more like women in Jamaica; she didn't ask questions about his business and was intelligent and easy to be with. She was also a good cook, an important asset to any Jamaican-born man.

On the chair to Charlie's right, D. was sipping his drink while he followed the intricate plot of the thriller playing on the TV screen. He and Jenny had come to the house earlier on and, after dinner, the two men had watched some videos and smoked while the women chatted and played with Marcus. Jenny was pregnant. She had announced the fact to D. one morning before leaving for work, but it was only when he woke up hours later that it hit him. Still, he didn't mind. He liked children, and having left three behind in Jamaica he welcomed the news as something to look forward to.

Charlie picked up the spliff he had left in the ashtray earlier and asked, 'Anyone we know got busted in the raid last night?'

D. shrugged. 'Only Shortie, and Jumbo of course . . .'

The two men laughed. Jumbo was an easy target. He was always high on crack, and always carried a small amount of drugs on him, as if he was afraid to be without for even a short time. That was why everybody called him Jumbo.

The raid on Shortie's place was a rare occurrence. Every illegal den had an arrangement of some sort with the police. Usually, this consisted of a certain amount of money being paid to a particular detective, regularly. The police in North London, as in all other areas, knew who was doing what and where. As long as there wasn't too much violence and everybody paid their dues, they didn't interfere with the business. They were mainly concerned with keeping the dealings in the Black areas. Should a white man get killed, or some smart youth try to establish himself outside the ghetto, it would be another matter. Shortie had probably been late with his payments, or maybe they needed some information from him.

'Shortie will soon be back in business,' Charlie said as he pulled on his spliff. 'All the same, it was a good thing you wasn't there last night.'

The two men concentrated on the movie for a while. Marcus had fallen asleep in Charmaine's arms. She took him upstairs to bed, Jenny followed her. Charlie made a few phone calls to some dealers to check when they would need more supplies. Business had been good these last few months. The merchandise kept coming through his contacts in America without problems. He sent couriers every three months or so and organized the processing and distribution according to a time scale, to minimize the losses in case any unforeseen accident should happen.

Things on the street had been quiet of late. Apart from the usual petty quarrels between hustlers, there was no major business-related conflict. The Spicers kept to their corners and D. did the same. No one had seen Blue since the incident outside Shortie's three months earlier. D. was looking out for him. He knew that it was only a matter of time.

Reports of the shoot-out had circulated throughout town and D. and the outfit were even more feared and respected as a result. They had recruited a few more soldiers and tightened the security, especially around the labs where the crack was processed.

The phone rang, drawing Charlie away from the movie. 'Yeah . . . Hey, man, what's happening . . .? What . . .?'

Alerted by the tone of Charlie's voice, D. turned towards him and noticed the frown on his face. After listening tensely for a few minutes, Charlie told the caller that he would get back to him and hung up. He was silent for a while. When he finally looked at D., his eyes were still, his face a weird mix of pain and anger.

'Is wha' happ'n?' D. enquired.

Charlie sighed heavily. When he spoke, his voice was cold as stone. 'Sherryl's dead . . . overdose.'

Aware that his friend was in shock, D. took his time and slowly managed to get the full story out of him. Sherryl, a beautiful light-skinned young woman in her twenties, was one of Charlie's couriers. She made two or three trips for him every year, bringing back about a pound of cocaine each time. He had known her for some time. They had been together at first but the relationship as lovers didn't last. However, they had stayed very good friends and Sherryl had been one of the first girls to fly to the US for Charlie. He had sent her to his people in New York the week before together with another girl and was expecting them back that day.

Sherryl had caused her own death. Instead of sticking to the instructions as she usually did, she decided this time to swallow a few condoms filled with base cocaine, to make a little more on the side. The rubber sheaths had burst in her stomach on the plane. She died of a massive overdose.

D. could see that his partner was affected by the news. Death was a common occurrence in the business they were in, but Sherryl was more than just a courier to Charlie. D. had met her a few times and got on fine with her. He felt bad about her death but there was nothing they could do now.

'What happened to the other girl?' D. asked.

Charlie always sent two couriers, with strict instructions to travel separately on the same return flight. In this way, the risk of both getting busted was minimum. Charlie shook himself out of his blues.

'She's OK . . . She was travelling in a different part of the plane. She didn't find out about Sherryl until they landed.'

They had only lost one load. The police would probably try and find out who Sherryl worked for, but this was no cause for worries. Charlie would make sure that there were no loose ends. Like most investigations into drug trafficking within the Jamaican community, this one would simply come to a dead end for lack of leads. Besides, the drugs found on Sherryl's body would just be added to the statistics of the yearly amount seized, the authorities would not make too much fuss about a dead black girl.

D. decided it was best to leave Charlie to his thoughts

for now. He just needed time to get over the shock, he would be fine. D. took his leave and went upstairs to inform Jenny that he would be back for her later.

'Better leave Charlie alone right now,' he told Charmaine. 'One business went wrong . . . Still, everyt'ing cool, don't worry.'

Charmaine knew better than to ask questions. D. left the house and got into his car. He knew High Noon was playing in Brixton, but it was yet too early for that. He didn't like to go to a dance before about three o'clock. He drove out towards Stoke Newington, hoping Sticks would be home. When he got to the estate, he noticed a noisy crowd on the first-floor landing of the block of flats where Sticks lived. D. parked the car and started up the stairs.

He climbed to the first floor, he heard shouts of anger and the voice of a screaming woman. A young girl was running down the stairs. He stopped her. 'Wha' ah gwan up deh?'

The girl seemed all excited. 'Some guy is trying to get into his girlfriend's flat to stab her,' she replied in a broad cockney accent.

D. left her and proceeded up the steps. On the landing, he had to push his way through a dozen people standing a few yards away from the scene of the action.

A young man was in front of the door to one of the flats. He shouted at someone inside the flat to let him in, while furiously kicking the door. In his right hand, the blade of a large cook's knife shone threateningly in the dim light of the landing. D. walked forward, calmly. Seeing that some new development was taking place, the noisy onlookers stopped their gossiping and watched. In his fury, the youth didn't notice D. immediately. He was about to unleash another violent kick in the door when he stopped, suddenly aware that the crowds had gone quiet.

He turned to his right and found himself staring at D. He raised the knife and shouted, 'Stay away from me, man!'

D. just stood there, looking at him. The youth registered the calm eyes, the expensive, well-cut clothes and the gleam of the gold rings and cargo. He could see the man was a Yardie. He lowered the blade and said: 'This has nothing to do with you, boss.'

Slowly, D. looked down at the big knife. He asked, 'Is what you wan' do with dat?'

'I'm gonna stab that fuckin' girl.' There was hatred in his voice. 'And nobody's gonna stop me.'

'So, wha' she do you?' D. asked, seemingly interested.

The youth frowned. He didn't know D., but couldn't figure out why a *ranks* like him was interested in a domestic quarrel. He looked at the door, then back at D. and said, 'She said she's ditching me for some other guy, but it's not going to happen . . .' The youth seemed confused. 'Look, man, leave me alone, right! This is between me and her.' He turned back towards the door.

D. called out to him as he was about to kick the door again. 'Star, tell me somet'ing; you wan' kill the girl or just cut her?'

The question, asked in a matter-of-fact tone of voice, hit the youth. He stood there with a puzzled look on his face, trying to think.

D. continued. 'The reason I ask . . . anyhow you stab her with dat deh lass, you good fe kill her, you know!'

The youth was listening, trying to see sense in the words.

D. shrugged. 'Anyway,' he told the youth, 'I gone now, I don't wan' to be here when the beas' dem come.'

He turned and started to walk away. The youth was still staring at him, his mind spinning fast. D. stopped and turned back towards him. 'Hear wha', I don't feel seh it's worth it to do time for a girl, seen?! 'Nough more ah dem out deh, star. Make she gwan, don't waste your life over dem t'ings deh, man.'

D. left the youth there and strolled back towards the stairs. The crowd made way for him, watching him in silence. As he climbed to the second landing, he heard an animated discussion begin below. He hoped his advice would avoid further disturbance and eventual bloodshed. Only a fool would do time over a woman.

Sticks opened the door for him. There was a broad grin across his face. He was on a high.

'Yes, don. Wha' you ah seh?'

'Cool, you know.'

D. walked in, following Sticks to the front room. The strong smell of crack explained the expression on Sticks' face. A girl was sitting on the carpet, staring at the TV screen. She muttered a vague greeting to D.

Sticks got two beers from the kitchen. D. told him of the incident downstairs at which they laughed heartily.

'I did hear some rumpus downstairs, but ah so dem deh people gwan all the while,' Sticks said.

He added that the youth was an idiot. He should have talked the girl into letting him inside the flat, and then stabbed her.

'So weh Charlie deh?'

D. told him of the death of Sherryl and that Charlie needed some time to cool off. He would make sure that everything was running fine. They talked business for a while, D. taking mental notes of the figures Sticks quoted concerning the week's takings. The girl was still glued to the TV, oblivious to everything else around her.

'I wan' you come to High Noon with me,' D. told Sticks.

Since the attempt on his life, Charlie had insisted that

D. should never be without at least one soldier to watch his back.

'Al'right, when you ready.'

Sticks was always willing to move with D.

They watched TV for a while. Sticks was restless; pacing up and down the flat, sitting down then getting up again. Finally, he went to the wall unit, took out a plastic carrier from one of the drawers, and sat down in front of the low wooden table. Out of the carrier, he carefully pulled out a black handgun in a paper bag. His face tense with concentration, he proceeded to load the gun. One by one he took short, shiny bullets from the paper bag and expertly inserted them into the ammunition clip from the gun. Once he had finished, he checked that the safety catch was on and, adjusting the weapon in his palm, he closed one eye and took careful aim at the girl. She didn't immediately realize what he was doing, engrossed as she was in the programme on the television. As she finally turned his way, she let out a frightened shriek.

'Don't mess about,' she cried, diving out of the way.

He teased her a little longer, following her in the weapon's sight as she desperately tried to find cover.

'How you so jumpy, man?' Sticks laughed.

He got up and slipped the gun in his belt. D. was ready now. Sticks put on his jacket and said to the girl, 'I gone out. You stay here till I come, seen?!'

The girl nodded in agreement and got back to watching TV. As the two men stepped outside, Sticks said to D, 'She kinda saaf, but she looks after me good.'

D. smiled. Sticks was a fast learner, he had set up himself nicely since coming over. He knew the soldier was loyal and brave. They went down the stairs. The incident on the first floor was over, everything was quiet.

On the way to Brixton, Sticks told D. of a rumour he

had heard on the street that Blue was staying out of town. By now, everyone knew that the tall soldier was behind the attempt on D. When neither he nor anyone from his outfit were present, hustlers and dealers debated the subject with passion. Some argued that the Spicers were too 'wicked' to be messed with while others defended D., pointing out that having escaped such an ambush in the first place, D. deserved respect. All agreed that the next encounter would be bloody.

'I can wait,' D. said after taking in the information. 'Him can run but him cyan hide.'

They passed Stockwell. High Noon was playing in a sound clash in a community hall, somewhere at the back of the High Street. D. didn't know the exact address, but it wouldn't be hard to find: Brixton was like a village where everyone knew everyone and everything going down. On the High Street, they followed a string of cars, identifiable by their occupants as heading for the dance.

On reaching the venue, there was nowhere to park. They took a few turns before finding a suitable space for the Mercedes in a dark street at the back of the petrol station.

Outside the hall, a noisy crowd was gathered in a formless queue. Cars were parked haphazardly almost right up to the door, groups of people talking and laughing. Ravers had come from every area to hear High Noon play Stylistic, a visiting Jamaican sound. A heavy bass was thumping its way right through the walls, spreading into the cold night air and guiding the late arrivals to the venue like a musical lighthouse.

D. and Sticks were making their way across the maze of vehicles, answering a few greetings, scanning the surroundings for known faces. As they passed a group of girls coming out of a car, Sticks passed one of them a flattering

87

remark. The girl smiled and answered something. Sticks stopped and started a conversation with her while her friends giggled around them. D. had stopped a few yards away. He waited patiently until Sticks got back to him, having made some form of date with the girl for later.

'Dat girl yah fit, you know,' Sticks said with a mischievous grin as they walked towards the crowded entrance.

D. shook his head, smiling.

'You sure seh you can handle dat,' he teased the slender youth, referring to the girl's size.

'How you mean, don,' Sticks retorted. 'You t'ink seh any girl can test me?!'

D. laughed. He let Sticks step in front of him to make a way through the crowd. Ignoring the shouts of protest, and cooling a few remarks with a cold stare, Sticks pushed and shoved until he found himself facing half a dozen burly bouncers. One put out his hand, intent on stopping the youth from going any further. Sticks stopped. Calmly, he stared into the bouncer's face.

'Where d'you think you're going?' the bouncer asked in an insolent voice.

Before Sticks had time to answer in kind, D. came from behind him and looked at one of the other large men blocking the way.

'Skipper, talk to your spar now!' he said coldly.

The crowd around them had fallen silent, hoping that maybe a confrontation would develop. The other bouncer said a few words into his friend's ear. Grudgingly, he stepped aside. D. walked in, followed by Sticks who made a point of throwing a cold look at the first bouncer.

'Dat bwoy better learn to show respect . . .' he said aloud.

Inside the hall, the temperature was high. D. looked

around him through the smoky haze. Stylistic was playing now, the music gushing from their stacks of speaker boxes spread strategically around the large room. The sound originated from the Denham Town area of Kingston, so D. knew most of their crew. Sticks leading the way, they proceeded slowly through the mass of sweating bodies towards the sound's control.

Skilly, the operator, saw D. first. From behind the set, he raised his hand in the air, index and middle fingers stuck out in the shape of a gun.

'Legal shots!' he shouted, beaming widely. 'Come in, don.'

The rest of the crew greeted D. and Sticks warmly. Skilly took the record off the turntable and deftly placed another one on. He dropped the needle on the acetate, let it spin for a few seconds then promptly lifted it up as the crowd noisily acknowledged the tune. The DJ sent some dedications, praised Stylistic briefly, then Skilly started the record again to popular approval. While the dancers went wild on the floor, Skilly said in D.'s ear, 'I hear seh you run into some trouble lickle while back . . .'

'Yeah, some business disagreement . . . Everyt'ing under control still . . .' D. replied above the noise.

Skilly and D. had spent two years in the same class way back during their primary school days. Although they had subsequently followed different paths, they had retained a strong bond and were happy to see each other so far away from home. As everything else happening in the Jamaican community anywhere in the world, D.'s story had circulated through the ghetto back home. Seeing that D. looked well and that he seemed confident in himself, Skilly didn't question him any further.

After asking Skilly about certain people back in Jamaica, D. left him to his work and headed for the bar, followed by Sticks. They bought some beers, pushed their way through to the back wall, and settled near one of the speakers. The atmosphere was hot, the crowd responding to the DJ's lyrics enthusiastically. D. took some herb, paper, and cigarettes out of his pockets and built a spliff, sprinkling a little white powder on the mix. Sticks did the same. They smoked and rocked to the sounds of Stylistic, tuning in to the general mood. Then it was High Noon's time. All the sound's faithful followers saluted the switch with whistles, horns, and shouts. The first record played provoked such an uproar that it had to be lifted up and started again three times. D. was enjoying himself as much as the rest of the dancers, though by habit he kept his back to the wall and regularly scanned the hall from underneath his half-closed eyelids. He felt Sticks nudge him.

'Dat same girl deh by the bar, I gwan check her out.'

The lanky youth made his way towards his date. D. stayed behind, smoking, and swaying to the rhythm. He was rocking to one of his favourite old-time tunes when he became aware of someone's eyes on him. He cast a seemingly casual look to his left, peering through the darkness and saw her. Twenty yards or so away, right by the corner of the wall and half-hidden by the bobbing heads of other dancers, Donna was staring his way. At first, he acted as if he hadn't seen her. He couldn't help but feel a little pinch of satisfaction inside.

He let a little time pass before he looked towards Donna again. As he turned his head, he saw her take cover behind a tall man, thinking he couldn't see her. He smiled to himself; so Donna was spying on him! He let her play hide-and-seek a little longer. The man behind whom she had been concealing herself moved away, leaving her exposed. D. looked straight at her and their eyes met.

Donna turned away fast. She just continued dancing for a few minutes, looking straight ahead. When she looked his way again, he motioned to her to come to him. She shook her head, too proud to obey. So he shrugged his shoulders not bothering to insist.

Seemingly unconcerned, D. lit up his spliff then took a sip from his drink. Rocking to the music, he scanned the dance hall. Sticks was nowhere to be seen. He was probably busy with the girl he went after. Finally, he turned to his left. This time Donna was staring at him insistently, she also seemed to have moved closer. He smiled at her and shook his head mockingly. She smiled back. Again, he called her to him, his eyes deep into hers. She looked away for a moment but, as he was tilting his head back to take another sip from his bottle, he saw her coming towards him. He kept his head straight and feigned surprise when she appeared by his side.

'You nah have no manners,' Donna said in his ear.

'Yeah? Well at least I don't spy 'pon you,' D. retorted.

Donna laughed and D. felt the old attraction he had always had towards her surface again. They talked for a while, exchanging jokes and light-hearted remarks. Stylistic had regained control of the dance. They spun several hot records, sending the crowd wild. The evergreen rhythm of that reggae classic 'The Whip' was currently enjoying one of its perennial comebacks, reliving the excitement of the original recording in a contemporary mix. A dozen or so reggae tunes qualified to be in the same immortal bracket as 'The Whip'. Tunes the rhythm of which Jamaicans refused to let die. Tunes which would be redressed and repackaged year after year. The Abyssinians', 'Satta Massagana', is another.

The sound's various resident MCs were taking turn to

tease the crowd, sending shivers of excitement down the dancers' spines as they matched audacious lyrics to Skilly's selection.

'Hear wha' . . .!' One of the Stylistic's top MCs asked for the record to be stopped. '. . . I don't wan' the people dem feel like it's a competition we ah play, you know!'

Then as the sound's followers whistled and shouted, he continued: 'No! I an' I jus' play music fe Black people, seen?!'

Skilly let the tune roll once again, sending the Studio One bass line straight to the ravers' heads. And once again, acknowledging the noisily expressed satisfaction of the public, he lifted it up. The MC took the opportunity of this break to send some dedications.

'Dis one goes to all the Yardman massives. Special request to the High Noon crew, also the promoter. And special request to D., I an' I long time brethren from Yard, from the Stylistic massive. Hold tight, don!'

Skilly let the record run all the way through this time. Donna looked up to D., a faint smile on her lips.

'So you ah de don now?!' she said.

'Ah me brethren dem, you know.'

Then, before she could go any further, he pulled her to him, gently. She fixed him for a brief moment, an undefinable look in her dark eyes, before letting her body rest against his. They started to rock. They danced right through the Studio One selection without speaking a word. Each of the songs brought them closer, their bodies sway-ing as one to the bounce of the bass. When they finally let go of each other, beads of sweat were trickling down their faces. They exchanged a brief look.

D. wiped his face and finished his beer. He asked her what she wanted to drink but, as he was about to head for the bar, he saw Sticks coming towards him through the crowd. He had a serious look on his face and didn't notice Donna at D.'s side.

'A man send me fe call you,' the youth told D.

D. frowned. It didn't sound like a joke. 'Who dat?' he asked.

'Chin find me near the bar, him ah wait fe you outside.'

D. scratched the back of his head. He turned to Donna. 'Wait fe me here, I' ha fe go meet a man.'

Donna simply nodded. D. followed Sticks towards the door. They went through the entrance and stepped outside. The cold air was a welcome relief after the steamy heat of the hall. D. looked around and spotted Chin standing alone near some cars.

'Make I see weh him ah seh,' he told Sticks.

D. walked up towards the man while his soldier sat on the bonnet of a car at a distance.

'How you do, Missa D.?' Chin said with a grin as D. approached him.

'Cool, you know.'

Suspicious, D. watched him closely, but Tony Chin seemed genuinely relaxed.

'I never know seh you ina dance, don,' D. said.

'Yeah man, I keep a low profile though, you know dem way deh?!' Chin finished his bottle of orange juice and dropped it on the ground.

'There are some t'ings you need to know, man,' he started. 'Some t'ings that only I is willing to tell you.'

D. looked into Chin's slanted eyes. The smile had vanished.

'You evah hear the name Gussie?' Chin asked.

D. shook his head negatively.

'Well, him dead now,' Chin continued, 'but Gussie was Blue's bigger brother. Him was Fox's right-hand man in the early days in Waterhouse. Fox sent him to Miami to work for me a little after I set up business there. Him couldn't stay ah Yard no more due to some trouble him did get into. I set up Gussie to collect from the dealers for me. Everything was cool for a while. I didn't know it at the time, but Gussie didn't want to work for the Spicers no more; as he reached foreign now, he decided to set up himself differently. So Gussie take himself one day and go rob one Colombian dealer in another area. After the war with the Cubans, we did agree to operate each one his own territory, some spots we left to the Colombians so dem wouldn't need to trouble nobody. Now Gussie went to the dealer to rob him and, as the guy tried to resist, shot him dead.'

Chin paused to light a cigarette. D. said nothing, waiting for him to go on. Chin looked at him briefly before resuming the story.

'I didn't know not'ing about that until Carly, one of my top soldiers, got shot in a restaurant in downtown Miami. Carly managed to make it back to my house, with five bullets ina him. Before he died, he told me that he was just leaving the place when three Colombians opened fire on him from a car. As Gussie was a Yardie, dem believed I was behind the killing of dem man. Now, I didn't know about Gussie's move, so I thought the Colombians dem wanted to start a war. Star, the way how me vex, I tracked dem down and killed couple ah dem myself. Carly and I was long time brethren, you know! Anyway, you must know the rest; the police locked me up for the killings and I did time. It's while I was inside that I learned the truth about Gussie. So I sent two orders to my man dem from jail: make peace with the Colombians . . . and deal with Gussie.'

Tony Chin stopped. He took a deep pull from his

cigarette, lost for a moment in his thoughts. D. waited and, as Chin was still silent after a few seconds, he asked: 'What is the connection with me?'

Chin was looking straight ahead. Finally, he looked at D. and said in a low voice, as if he didn't want anyone else to hear: 'Fox couldn't say not'ing. He knew Gussie's killing was business, not personal. Blue knows about the story. Him vex but him not mad enough to try anyt'ing with me.'

D. was listening, interested by the revelation but unable to see what it all had to do with him. He was about to question Chin further when the man leaned closer towards him.

'It was Gussie who killed your brother . . .' Chin said softly.

D. stood there, motionless, as the information sank into his brain. He stared coldly at Chin for a minute, looking for something that could make him doubt the man's words. There had been so much speculation as to the identity of Jerry's killer that he found it hard to accept the truth. The story sounded real, and it would explain why no one was willing, or able, to tell him anything, even years after. Those who knew that Jerry's killing was down to the Spicers were not prepared to talk. Even Skeets, D.'s mentor in the organization, had preferred to keep the truth from him.

As Chin explained the circumstances behind Jerry's death, D. found himself back in the steamy atmosphere of the West Kingston streets. True to his new life, Jerry was firmly opposed to the drug trafficking that had started to swamp Jamaica. Situated as it is between South America the producer and the United States the consumer, the island had quickly become a transit point for the cocaine trade. The Bahamas, the original stop-over, were too exposed by then, and covered by the US Drug Enforcement

Agency. Cocaine offered the means of making big money, and a sure route to a better life in the States for thousands of Jamaican youths. Almost overnight, it became as readily available as the locally produced ganja.

To a God-loving, clean-living Rastaman like Jah Jerry, cocaine was a devilish invention, manufactured by the white man to maintain Black people in a state of mental slavery. It brought nothing but suffering and death. Though Jerry realized fully the extent of the problem and the power of the gangs involved in the trade, he constantly preached against the evil of the drug and intended to keep his community off-limits to the drug barons and their pushers. So when the Spicers sent a few soldiers to establish a retail operation in the Maxfield Avenue neighbourhood, they encountered a stiff resistance from the tall Dreadlocks. One afternoon, as they were trying to entice some youngsters to try a cocaine spliff, the Spicers were cornered by Jerry and a handful of his brethren. There was an angry exchange of words and in front of a sizeable crowd, Jerry chased the pushers out of the area, warning them that should they dare return, they would face the wrathful judgement that they rightly deserved. One morning three weeks later, Jerry was found dead in an alley just off Lyndhurst Road. He had been stabbed several times in the chest and throat.

'Why you tell me dis now?' D. asked after a while.

He found it hard to believe Chin didn't have good reason for speaking out.

'We have a common enemy, star. Blue would rather make sure you dead before you learn the truth. Maybe Fox ordered the hit on you, maybe he didn't . . . . Like how you ah get big now, dem don't feel safe. Even if you didn't rob dem, sooner or later dem would have to come after you.'

he smell of fried salt fish and onions was still in
the air. Sitting at the wooden kitchen table,
Jenny was finishing her plate. Opposite her,
Charmaine was trying to convince Marcus to eat
the piece of dumpling she had dipped in the
stew for him. But the little boy was in a playful
mood; he teasingly opened his mouth and
quickly closed it as soon as the food was within
reach. After each unsuccessful attempt by his
mother, he mockingly threw her a mischievous sideways
glance. Charmaine was patient with her son. Eventually
she got him to eat enough until he firmly refused any more
food.

Standing at the sink, Sweetie was through washing-
up. She was Charlie's first cousin and had arrived in
England seven years earlier while he was still living in New
York. She and Charmaine had got on well from the start
and they visited each other's house regularly. Marva,
known to everyone as Sweetie because of her small size,
was a tiny and attractive dark woman in her late twenties.
Born in Spanish Town, she had emigrated to Canada with
her parents at an early age, returning to live in Jamaica
several years later due to an unfortunate incident involving
the stabbing of a fellow countrywoman. Sweetie's easy-
going ways and pleasant smile belied a fiery temper . . .
Finally, after a couple of years in her old neighbourhood,
she opted to go and live in England where life was similar
to what she was used to in Canada. Charlie and Sweetie

were close, she had helped him to settle when he first arrived in the country.

Charmaine and Jenny had arrived at Sweetie's house early that morning, having arranged to spend the day together. Charlie had left for the States a few days earlier to settle some business. After lunch, the three women settled in Sweetie's comfortable living room, watching television and chatting. On the screen, a popular soap opera unfolded its usual tale of romance and extra-marital affairs. There was silence for a while as Marcus fell asleep and the three women followed the predictable plot of the show.

'Dem deh woman nah easy!' Sweetie remarked, commenting on the adulterous behaviour of one of the television characters.

'Well her marriage is not working out,' Jenny said defending the woman in question.

Sweetie kissed her teeth to express her contempt for the show. 'I don't usually watch dem t'ings, you know. Too much foolishness ah gwan.'

'Most women follow this one,' Charmaine said.

'True, some ah my friends watch it too . . . But I cyan bother with dat.' Sweetie stressed her point. 'A woman musn't gwan dem way deh.'

'What do you mean?' Jenny asked.

The show was drawing to a close, but the women's attention was on the debate it had sparked. Sweetie explained. 'Why the woman cyan done with her husband first before jumping into bed with a next man? I don't respect dem kind ah t'ings.'

'You're right,' Charmaine said, 'but that happens a lot over here. And these soap operas influence people to an extent.'

Sweetie leaned to take the carton of orange juice on

the table in front of her and poured some in the glasses. 'Dat is what I'm saying,' she said after taking a drink. 'You find all the young girls dem taking it in and doing the same t'ing.'

'So what about when a man go and have another woman besides his own?' Jenny asked, taking the discussion a step further.

Charmaine smiled and said nothing. She waited for Sweetie's answer.

'Well, dat's wrong, but a woman must know how to cope with dese problems.' Sweetie paused. 'Also it depends what type of situation it is.'

Jenny didn't agree. For her there was no redeeming aspect to a man's infidelity.

'Well, to me it makes no difference. If a man messes about you can't stay with him.'

Sweetie laughed.

'That is how the majority of women think over here,' Charmaine said.

'And wha you ah seh?' Sweetie asked her.

'I used to think like that, you know, but I found that most men keep more than one girlfriend,' Charmaine answered.

Sweetie nodded. 'Dat is how Black man stay. Weh me ah seh is dat you must check whether a man jus' ah sport or if him face him responsibility.'

Jenny asked: 'So, you're not jealous?'

Sweetie looked at her, serious. 'Me jealous, yes . . . but I also know dat you cyan cage a man.' She continued: 'What matters to me is dat my man treats me with respect. Now, I expect him to provide for me and the children dem. As long as him don't neglect him family, whatever him do outside is up to him. Still, him better be careful I don't find out not'ing, else I will confront him with it.'

Jenny looked unconvinced by the argument. 'I still can't accept another woman taking away my man.'

Sweetie laughed. 'Mek I tell you somet'ing, Jenny . . .' she said, looking at her. 'No woman can force a man to do t'ings him don't wan' fe do.'

Charmaine had kept silent, leaving her two friends to battle it out. She understood Jenny's way of thinking, having been born and bred in England herself, but she also knew that there was no easy answer to that age-old man/woman argument.

'One thing I found out,' she said, 'Jamaican men check other girls but they do look after their main woman. They will go out and make sure they get money to provide for their family.'

Sweetie agreed. 'True; you see in Jamaica, a man cyan keep a woman if he don't look after her good. A woman tend to cling to her man dem way deh.'

'So what about the women, don't they want to earn money for themselves?' Jenny asked.

'How you mean?!' Sweetie retorted. 'Den you nah see how Yard woman love hustling?'

'It's true . . .' Jenny conceded.

Sweetie went on. 'T'ings different in Jamaica, you know! From you grow as a youth, you have to find some ways to earn some dollars, 'cause you cyan expect too much, even from your parents dem.'

The selection of cartoons on the television screen were without an audience, because Marcus, the only person in the room who would have enjoyed them, was still sound asleep on the sofa.

'Ouno lucky down here,' Sweetie explained, 'from a woman have a child the State looks after her, gives her a flat and money weekly. In Jamaica, if you don't have a man to help you, t'ings rough.'

Charmaine nodded, then added, 'You're right, but that makes women lazy in a way.'

The women went on discussing the respective merits of life in Britain and in Jamaica a while longer. So animated was the debate that they didn't notice at first when Marcus woke up. He soon made himself heard though. Finally, seeing that a timid sun had poked its face outside, they decided to go for a walk in the nearby park.

'We can take some pictures,' Sweetie said, picking up her new camera.

'I'm not dressed for that!' Jenny objected, conscious of her bulging shape.

Her friends laughed, teasing her.

'If you wanted to do modelling, you shouldn't get involved in baby-making . . .!'

They went out in the warm afternoon. It looked like spring was coming early this year.

Shots whistled close . . . too close. The dull impact of large bullets against the walls and the scream of shattered glass . . . Shadows passed in front of the window . . . dark shapes with barrels threateningly pointing towards the house. D. felt the familiar tightening of the stomach, the dry throat . . . thoughts racing through his brain. Then the shrill sound of an approaching siren, very near, right behind the shot-riddled door. D. waited, tense as a bow-string, frantically trying to figure a way out of the trap. There had to be a way out, there always was. The siren wailed persistently, covering all other noises and drilling through D.'s mind. Suddenly, the door exploded in a cloud of dark smoke . . . but the siren didn't stop . . . D. jumped up, ready to make a run for it, his last run. He opened his eyes and recognized the poster of the grinning dreadlocked child on the bedroom wall. The door bell kept ringing . . .

Blowing out air from between his parched lips, D. wiped the beads of sweat from his brow and got up. Unsteadily, he made his way to the door. He saw Sticks' scarred profile through the peephole. He opened up, let him in, and put the lock back on.

'How you love ring people's bell so, man,' D. muttered, stepping into the living room.

'Den nah you tell me fe come check you, Don?' Sticks laughed.

All the same, D. was glad he had been awakened from the nightmare. He sat on the sofa straightening his thoughts.

'Look like you did have a rough night,' Sticks remarked, dropping his long frame into one of the leather chairs.

'Hmm . . . rough, yes; I go over by Kelly. Him spar, Carl, jus' come out ah jail. Man, we base excess amount ah charlie last night . . . and drink champagne too. Ev'rybody mash up!'

D. himself still looked 'mash up'! He got up and went to switch on the stereo. The loud beat of a live session cassette blasted through the room. Scratching his head, he stood in the middle of the room, as if unsure where he was and what he should do. He spun around, glancing rapidly over the shelves against the wall before heading out of the room, mumbling to himself. He came back in almost right away, frowning. Finally, he turned to Sticks.

'Wha'ppen? You have anyt'ing?'

Sticks searched his inside pocket and brought out two small plastic bags which he handed to D. Taking them, D. went back out and returned with a small glass pipe. He sat in front of the table and proceeded to load the small piece of white rock from one bag inside the open glass pipe. Sticks passed him a lighter and he struck it, placed the high flame against the mouth of the tube and pulled sharply. Thick, white smoke flew up the pipe, enveloping D. in a cloud. A few more pulls and D. leaned back in the chair, the pipe still in his hand. The frown on his face had been replaced by a frozen half-grin. Sticks hadn't moved; he was nodding mechanically to the rhythm of the music, throwing occasional glances in D.'s direction.

Without realizing it himself, D. had been using cocaine, and especially crack, more and more frequently in the last few months. Of course, no one around him would have dared mention it to him, but he had become increasingly moody and ignorant. Even Donna who had experienced the change in him at first-hand, hadn't been able to discuss the subject with him. He was often so tense and quick-tempered that she didn't want to risk an argument by saying the wrong thing at the wrong time. Also, because he was now the 'top man' in the area, D. felt practically almighty. He was the ruling king, and all the hustlers and players were his subjects and acting as such. Whether through love or through fear, everyone respected D. The constant praises and flattery of the army of sycophants who watched his every move only added to the inflated view he had of himself.

'One girl, named Lisa, was looking for you down Rocco's last night . . .' Sticks said after a while.

D. had heard his lieutenant, but he took almost a full minute to answer. Slowly, he turned towards Sticks.

'Lisa . . .?'

'Yeah man; browning, tall and slim . . .'

D. remembered. He kissed his teeth dismissively. 'Me have dat already, star; a deadstock . . .'

D. seemed to have recovered. Gone was the exhausted

103

look and the foul mood. He was fresh again. He got up, stretched, then went to turn the tape over. Finally, after a quick look out of the window, he headed for the bathroom. The soldier, meanwhile, was still rocking hypnotically to the beat of the music. The thin, scarred face didn't betray any expression. Sticks had not moved a muscle when D. reappeared twenty minutes later, dressed and carrying his mobile phone. He went to the kitchen and brought back a carton of orange juice and two glasses.

'So, how the rounds go?' he asked after pouring out some juice and taking a sip.

Sticks pulled himself out of his trance and took out a leather pouch from inside his jacket. He handed it to D. and gave him the report of the dealers' checks he had done earlier that morning. D. listened, mentally recording the amounts outstanding and evaluating the supply requirements in each case.

He reflected that they had enough processed crack in the lab to last maybe until the following week. Charlie was due back from New York at the end of the month but he would send back the two couriers he had travelled with, ahead of his flight. He would surely call in the next few days.

They had been making good money. Every member of the outfit was paid more than enough to avoid, as Charlie said, 'the temptation of getting careless'. The reason their operation was going so well was that it employed a minimum amount of people and was run with maximum security. There was no direct contact between Charlie and D. and the street dealers who worked for them. The security teams for the lab consisted of hand-picked soldiers who only reported to Sticks and Indian. Also, none of those working in the team was foolish enough to risk incurring D.'s wrath. His reputation alone kept everything running smoothly.

would be pleasantly surprised to find dinner ready. the case with most men who grow up in Jamaica, cooking had been part of D.'s upbringing. He had improved with time and practice and, by all accounts, he was now quite good at it. However, his style of life nowadays left little time for such activities. Yet today he had summoned all of his culinary skills to impress Donna. And it worked!

Following their chance meeting at the Stylistic dance a few months earlier, the pair had gotten back together. The attraction they had always had towards each other was strong, too strong to resist. While they had been apart, D. knew within himself that he had missed her as much as she had missed him. Only pride had stopped him from going back. Donna knew about Jenny and the baby she was expecting. She told D. she didn't care about that. As far as she was concerned he was her man and no 'English gal' could take him away.

Cindy, Donna's daughter, had enjoyed the dinner too. She sat between D. and her uncle Leroy, watching television. She had taken to D. easily, focusing on him all the affection a child needs to give her father. He got on fine with Cindy too, treating her like he would the daughter of the same age he had left back in Jamaica. D. always laughed at the way she beamed with pride and waved at her friends on the block whenever he took her for a drive in his car. With Donna and Cindy, D. could relax and express the caring, softer side of his personality that no one else knew.

'I wan' come check you for some cassettes,' D. said to Leroy.

'Some fresh selection due fe reach next week. I will bring dem up for you.'

'Al'right.'

Donna was in the kitchen, clearing up and doing the washing-up. The phone rang.

'Cindy! See who it is . . .' Donna called out.

The child got up and ran to the phone. She came back into the room after a few seconds.

'D., it's someone for you!' Cindy shouted.

D. went out of the room to the phone. He reflected that it could only be Sticks. He picked up the receiver. It was Indian.

'Respect, don. Sticks tell me whe' you deh. I have somet'ing dat might interest you.'

'Like wha'?' D. asked.

'Well, hear dis. The bwoy you ah look for . . .? I get him baby mother address from one of my girls.'

D.'s features hardened somewhat but his voice was the same when he asked, 'Tell me now . . .?!'

Indian gave him a name and an address, somewhere in north-west London. D. scribbled it on the pad from the phone table.

'I appreciate dat, me breddah.'

He thanked Indian, then asked: 'Sticks deh wid you . . .? Let me talk to him.'

When he got his soldier on the phone, D. told him to go to the address Indian had just given him and watch the place. He was to take Linton with him and call as soon as the girl showed up. 'Ouno just keep out of sight, seen?! Wait dere and report to me on the mobile.'

When he had finished speaking, D. folded the piece of paper with the address and put it in his pocket. By the time he sat back down on the sofa, his face had returned to its neutral expression.

'So when you ah fly out?' D. asked Leroy.

'I book a flight for July. My brethren will take care ah de shop till I return.'

'People will be shock to see you again, man!' D. laughed.

107

'True,' Leroy said thoughtfully. 'I never did t'ink seh I would be gone for so long.'

'Ah so it go, you know. Once you reach ah foreign, you can never tell how long before you come back.' D. paused, then went on. 'It's only t'rough money most people leave. Aside from dat nowhere nah better than Yard.'

Leroy and D. talked for a while about Jamaica, reminiscing about their days in West Kingston, the friends they had left behind and the excitement of the warm nights spent at local dances or in the backyards of their neighbourhood. As they spoke, a nostalgia crept upon them. How far away it all seemed . . .!

Finally, Leroy took his leave. Outside, night had fallen on the town.

Cindy was asleep between the two men. Donna took her to bed.

D. was staring absent-mindedly at the TV when she returned. She sat beside him and tried to get him to talk but his mind was somewhere else, far away.

He barely noticed when she retired to her room. Images of the past were drifting through his mind. Happy times, familiar faces, days and nights of excitement and danger, hazily intermingled. He remained there, alone in the semi-darkness, oblivious to the low buzzing sound of the television, until the high-pitch ring of his cellular phone interrupted the dream.

'D., weh you deh?' Sticks' voice brought him back to the present.

'Still deya, wha'ppen?'

'Hear wha'; two girls come in a while ago with a pickney, one a dem jus' lef, must be a friend . . .'

'Al'right, I comin' now. Which part dat place deh?'

Sticks explained briefly the quickest way to get to the address they were watching. D. told him to wait there, then he called Robbie at his house. The big soldier sounded sleepy but said that he would be ready any time. D. went to the bathroom to wash his face, then to the kitchen for a glass of fruit juice. He put on his shoes and jacket and, before leaving, peeped into the bedroom. Donna was asleep, with Cindy's arm around her; he closed the door silently, and went out.

Once in the car, he checked his watch, changed the tape in the stereo, and headed for Stamford Hill to pick Robbie up. The night was mild, with people walking leisurely alongside the main road, going home or strolling with friends. It was one of those warm nights that make people from overseas long for their homeland, star-studded skies and the gentle brushing noise of the ocean against the shore.

He got to Robbie's house and rang the bell. The door opened almost immediately. He walked in, greeted the soldier who, though fully dressed, had visibly not long woken up.

'How you love sleep so, man!?' D. teased him.

'Bwoy, you wan' see . . . a youth gimme a draw earlier on, and from I get home I jus' feel fe rest, you know . . .'

'So wha'ppen, none ah it nah lef?'

Robbie smiled. D. followed him into the living room and started to build a spliff.

After a few draws, D. realized what Robbie meant. It was prime sensimilla, dark green with a rich smell, the kind that was so rare in England nowadays. Remembering he had some business at hand, D. shook himself out of the relaxed mood that had begun to creep up on him.

'Come now, Sticks ah wait fe me.'

As they drove out, he told Robbie of Indian's tip. The soldier laughed, happy to get on Blue's trail, for whom he kept a solid grudge.

'You feel seh de bwoy stay dere?' he asked expectantly.

D. shrugged.

'It don't matter fe now. Cyan catch Bwoy Blue, ketch fe him t'ing . . .'

They laughed wickedly. D. lit the spliff, took a pull, then passed it to Robbie. At this late hour, there wasn't much traffic on the road and they soon reached Kilburn. Sticks had explained that the girl lived on one of the roads off the High Street. D. found it easily.

'See dem deh!' Robbie said when they were half-way down the tree-lined road.

Sticks' car was parked on the left, all lights off. As they passed it, the bass from the stereo bounced up to them from the open window. D. parked in a vacant space a little further up. They got out and walked back. There were large Victorian three-storey houses on both sides of the road. Except for a few passing cars and the barking of a lonely dog in a nearby garden, it was all quiet.

'How it stay?' D. asked, once they had climbed in the back of Sticks' car.

'She must be in bed. The light on the first floor out now,' the soldier explained, pointing out at a window across the road.

'She one in deh?'

'And her pickney . . .'

D. was silent for a while, looking at the house.

'What you wan' do, don?' Sticks asked.

'You and Linton wait here . . . I gwan leave a message,' D. said cryptically. He looked at Robbie. 'Hear wha'; you ring the bell, I maas under the porch. When she look out the window, you tell her you have a message from Blue. If she ask anything more, tell her seh him get arrested, you ha fe talk to her urgently, seen?'

Robbie nodded. They got out and crossed over to the

other side. When they reached the house, Robbie pushed the gate open and they climbed the few steps. Everything was quiet. The soldier rang the bottom bell while D. stood in the shadow of the dimly lit street door. After a few seconds, there was a knock at the first-floor window. Robbie looked up and motioned to the silhouette behind the glass to open. The sash window slid up and the girl stuck her head out, looking puzzled.

'Sis, Blue send me . . . somet'ing happened . . .' Robbie did his best to sound convincing.

'What's wrong? Where is he . . .?' The voice sounded sleepy, worried but not suspicious.

'Dem hold him . . . you ha fe help him . . .' Robbie played his part perfectly.

D. heard the sound of the window closing down. Robbie looked at him and nodded, smiling. They heard footsteps coming from inside the house, then the door of the flat opening. D. drew back against the wall to the left, out of sight. Through the thick, wired glass he could see the form of a woman dressed in a loose gown, hurrying down the corridor. Slowly, he took out the knife from his back pocket and opened it. He stood still, the blade low against his leg. The door was unlocked from inside. Robbie stayed in full view.

'What's happening?' The girl had opened the door and was looking at Robbie.

D. didn't wait for his soldier to answer. He jumped out of the shadow and stepped in, simultaneously grabbing the girl by the hair and sticking his blade right against her throat.

'One sound and you gone . . .' he whispered in her ear.

The girl's eyes were wide open with surprise and shock. She took a sharp breath and swallowed, fear written

111

all over her face. Meanwhile, Robbie had closed the street door.

'Inside!' D. commanded.

They walked to the flat, Robbie in front, his knife held at the ready, while D. pushed the trembling girl in ahead of him. They entered. Robbie closed the door.

'Who else in deh?' D. asked the girl once they were inside.

'Only my son . . .' Her breath was short, the head tilted away as far as she could from the knife. 'What do you want?'

'Weh Blue deh?'

'I don't know . . . I haven't seen him since last week . . .'

D. pressed the tip of the knife against the girl's neck. Her breath accelerated.

'Please . . . It's the truth . . . I swear . . .'

D. looked into her eyes; she was too scared to lie. He motioned to Robbie to check upstairs. While the soldier was gone, D. shoved the girl into the adjoining living room and pushed her on to a chair. His knife still at the ready, he looked at her closely for the first time since she had opened the door. The room was dark. Only the light from the corridor threw shadows around them. She was rather pretty, in her early twenties, with shoulder-length black hair and a large mouth. Her dark brown complexion and straight nose showed she was a *coolie*, as people of Indian ancestry are called in Jamaica. She sat there, frozen in the armchair. Though she knew nothing about him, she could tell a man like D. would kill her without hesitation if he had reason to.

'What's your name?' D. asked in a cold voice.

'Rita . . .' she managed to say through parched lips. Then: 'Please don't hurt my son . . .'

112

'Shut up, gal!' D. ordered. 'Is Blue pickney?'

The girl didn't answer; she was afraid for her child more than for herself. Robbie came back down.

'Only the youth up deh . . . Him ah sleep.'

D. looked at the girl. 'So you don't wan' tell me weh your man deh?'

He pointed the sharp blade towards her face. The girl tried to draw away from it with a terrified sound, but there was nowhere to go.

'Please . . . I don't know anything . . . He only comes see his son sometimes . . .'

D. frowned and looked at Robbie.

'Mek we kill her and done,' the big soldier said in a flat voice.

D. didn't want to spend too much time in the house. He grinned at Robbie, then to the girl.

'I want you to give your man a message from me . . .'

With his left hand he grabbed Rita by the front of her nightdress and pulled downwards. The flimsy garment tore under his grip. The girl started a sound, quickly repressed by the threat of the knife against her throat. D. pulled her by the arm and threw her on the floor. He read in the girl's terrified eyes that she knew what he was going to do.

'Oh no! Please . . .' she begged, tears rolling down her cheekbones.

'Shut your mouth! Or you wan' dead?'

Quickly, D. pulled aside what was left of the nightdress. Although afraid for her life, the girl tried to stop him from taking off her underwear. Swearing, D. slashed her sharply on her right hand. She made an attempt to scream, and he slapped her face with the back of his left hand. A small trickle of blood appeared at the corner of her mouth. After that she stopped fighting. She lay there whimpering

113

faintly as he took her and satisfied himself. Robbie, standing in the doorway, was smiling.

D. got up and fixed himself up. He looked down at the girl. She was crying softly as she tried to gather her torn garments to cover herself.

'Tell Blue I wan' see him!' D. said in a matter-of-fact tone of voice. 'Don't forget . . .'

Robbie opened the door of the flat and they stepped out. Quietly, they went out of the house and walked back to Sticks' car.

'Al'right, check me ah morning,' D. told Sticks.

'So . . . wha'ppen?' Sticks asked him, as he turned to get back to his car.

D. turned around briefly, grinning. 'I just gave her a message for Blue.'

Robbie laughed, nodded to Sticks, and followed D.

The narrow bunk was about three feet away, with a ragged and dirty mattress. From the ceiling a bulb threw its bleak white rays around the cell. As cold as the tiled floor was, it was nothing compared to the chill Barry felt creeping in his bones. He wasn't sure how long he had been there, sitting in the corner opposite the door, his arms around his folded legs. They had taken his watch, along with his belt and shoe laces. He brought his numb fingers up to his face and blew on them in a futile attempt to warm them up. Inside the trainers, his toes were so cold that he could feel them no more.

Wiping tiny beads of sweat from his brow, Barry listened out for any noises coming from outside the cell door, but nothing. Only the hostile silence. He had told them about his condition before they locked him up. He knew it wouldn't be long before the dreaded pain started to play hide-and-seek in his stomach. The two young officers had laughed and called him a 'dirty junkie'.

'We'll leave you alone for a while, son. Maybe after that you can tell us something useful,' the sergeant had said with a sympathetic look.

Yet, no matter how much Barry had racked his brain, he could think of nothing that would convince the policemen to let him go. It wasn't the first time . . . Now and again, they would pick him up, wherever they found him, to squeeze little bits of information out of him. The fear of the oncoming pain was making him sick, even before the actual withdrawal symptoms had begun to torment his whole body, turning him into a sweating, crying wretch, crawling on the floor like a wounded animal.

It was the third time this month that they had arrested him, for no other reason than that he was an obvious target for the tips-hungry officers. Faced with a spate of drugs-related violent crimes, the police had a habit of extracting information out of vulnerable people like Barry. He shivered. Things had not always been that bad. For several years, he made a living out of dealing hash, amphetamines, and acid. He had his problems at times, but he was smart and usually managed to keep out of the police's net. Everything changed for the worse however, when he started to get involved with heroin, or smack as it was called out on the streets. Vince, a white friend from school-days whom he hadn't seen for years, had introduced him to that line of work. They met by chance in a Camden pub one Saturday night. They had been close during their childhood, running the streets and later chasing girls together. Although Vince was white, he had always been straight with him and the two boys struck a durable friendship. Barry was glad to see Vince again after such a long time.

So, how're you doing, son?' Vince asked after a few drinks.

'All right, you know . . . just doing a little business here and there.'

Vince smiled, the same mischievous smile he had at school.

'Getting rich, are you?'

'Not really, just making ends meet.' Barry threw an admiring glance at Vince's smart clothes.

'You seem to be doing fine . . .'

Vince smiled modestly. He offered Barry a cigarette

then, leaning towards him, said, 'If you're interested, I could turn you on to something, you know wha' I mean . . .?'

'I might be . . . it depends.' Barry was curious.

'It's a good earner, if you're smart . . .' Vince winked at his old friend.

'Tell me more . . .' Barry said.

Vince paid for the drinks and they went out. Later that night, Barry returned home with a small bag of smack he took from Vince on trust. He thanked his luck, convinced that his life was about to change. It did . . .

Dealing heroin was fine to begin with. Barry was introduced to a few contacts and, within a couple of weeks, he was able to repay Vince and buy more stuff from him. He got new customers. Money was turning faster than before. He sold mostly to white youths, who trusted him because he was Vince's friend, and they liked the merchandise. He took the habit of snorting, to test the quality of what he was selling. It was a different feel from what he was used to, but it didn't seem to affect him too badly at first, so he thought nothing of it.

Looking back from where he was now, sick and trembling, Barry couldn't really explain how it all happened. Following some of his new friends, he shot the drug up his arm, once . . . Within six months he was totally hooked, living through, and for, the drug. From then on it all went downwards, like an infernal spiral which brought him lower than he thought a man could descend. After a while, he found that he couldn't trade any more, as he had begun to feed his expensive habit from his own supply. He was soon in debt to Vince, his friend, who showed little sympathy for his condition and refused to give him any more heroin on credit. He made promises he knew he couldn't keep, pleaded and begged until Vince told him in no uncertain terms he wanted nothing more to do with him. Barry had become a liability.

A cramp gripped his stomach and he retched. Getting down on his hands and knees, he tried to push himself upright but his body was weak. He could feel sweat running down his spine, under his armpits, all over his shivering frame. Another spasm threw him down on to the cold floor. The thought of his own death, in this lonely cell, took shape in his mind. Barry turned and rolled on his back. The glare of the bulb burned his eyes through the tears. He knew he needed to get out fast, to get some help. Most of all he needed a shot to escape the torture.

Suddenly, a thought flashed through his head, a few remembered words in a flash of lucidity. He forced himself to think, his forehead pressed against the cold floor. He had something . . . something he could throw to his tormentors. It wasn't much, just a bit of conversation overheard a few days before, but he had nothing to lose. At that precise moment, Barry would have sold his own mother if he thought that could get him out. Gathering what little strength he had left, he got on his knees and half-crawled towards the door. With cramps tugging at his bowels ever more regularly and a bilious taste in his mouth, he made it to the steel door. He banged on the door with his fists, as hard as he could, calling out. After what seemed to him like hours, he heard some footsteps, the sound of heavy boots on the tiled floor, getting closer and closer. He banged some more.

'Open up . . . please. I need to see someone.' His voice was a hoarse whisper.

He heard the click of the key inside the lock, then felt a gush of air on his face. He looked up. It was one of the officers who had taken him in.

'Look at the state of you!'

'I want to talk to you . . . I've got something.'

The young policeman could see that Barry was sick. Gripping him by the collar, he pulled him up. Barry steadied himself, holding on to the wall, breathing heavily.

'All right, come on!'

The officer pulled him along the corridor, then inside the room he had been in earlier. Exhausted, fighting against the rising nausea, Barry dropped in a wooden chair. The young policeman opened the door leading to the next room, where his colleague was conducting another interrogation. Barry heard some shouted questions, then a voice answering in a heavy Jamaican accent. The officer came back, closed the door and sat at the table.

'See what you doing to yourself! More of that junk and you'll soon be dead.'

Barry wiped his face with a trembling hand. 'I feel sick . . . you got to let me out.'

The officer shook his head in pity, or disgust, then got up and went to the table in the corner of the room. He poured out some coffee from a jug into a plastic cup, and placed it in front of Barry.

'Here, drink this!'

Barry took the cup with both hands and took a mouthful of the lukewarm, bitter liquid. He coughed violently as the coffee went down inside his stomach.

'Right . . .' the officer said, 'what you got for us, then?'

Barry finished the coffee and took a deep breath. Leaning towards the officer, he said: 'I know where you can find a lab . . .'

'A lab?'

'You know . . . a crack house.' Barry coughed again.

'Oh, yeah?! And where is this lab then?'

The policeman didn't seem to take the information

119

seriously. Barry gave him the location of the lab, trying to sound as convincing as possible. While he was speaking, he felt the familiar jabbing sensation inside and tensed himself, his hands gripping the edge of the table in front of him. He breathed deeply.

'This estate is a big place. You've got to do better than that.' The officer shook his head.

'I'm telling you all I know, honest!' Barry pleaded, a sincere look in his eyes.

He was scared at the thought that they might put him back in the cell. Patiently, he repeated the information, insisting that the flat would be easy to find.

'You've been there before, have you?' the officer enquired.

'No. No one can go to the house, but I heard these guys talking about it.' Barry was playing his best card. 'It's a door with some security railing on the first landing.'

The officer sighed and scratched his head. He got up and walked to the next room. When he came back, the sergeant was with him.

'So that's all you can tell us, eh?' The policeman towered over Barry, shirt sleeves rolled up, his large stomach protruding over his trousers belt.

'It's a good tip, gov . . . I've got nothing else, I swear.' Barry's voice trembled with fear and pain.

The sergeant let out a deep, ugly laugh. 'You swear! You think I believe anything coming from a dirty junkie like you?! I know your kind; all liars and thieves. All you wogs are the same . . .'

There was a threat in his voice. Barry bowed down his head, knowing he just had to let the storm pass. He would bear any insult as long as they let him out.

The big policeman looked at him for a while in open disgust.

'If you send us on a wild-goose chase, we'll get back to you, you know that?!'

Barry nodded in silence.

'All right, let him go,' the sergeant said finally, before going back to his other victim next door.

Sighing with relief, Barry followed the young policeman out. As they passed the half-open door of the adjoining room, his eyes met with those of a young man sitting at a table, handcuffed. The contact didn't last more than three seconds, yet Barry felt the depth of the stare from the dark cold eyes.

In the foyer, he got back his few possessions and headed for the large glass doors leading outside. Before he reached them, he heard the young officer's voice behind him.

'See you later . . .'

Barry didn't turn back. He stepped out of the station, down the few steps and into the sunny street. He walked fast, needled by the recurring jabs in his stomach. He knew what he needed, and he needed it fast . . .

The sound of the television was high enough to be heard from outside. D. turned the key in the lock and opened the door to the flat. He walked in, closed the door behind him, and entered the living room. Jenny and Carol, her older sister, were sitting on the sofa, watching a programme. D. muttered a greeting. Carol looked up and answered him but Jenny only glanced towards him with a frown. D. could tell by the way she glared at the screen that she was in a foul mood. He decided to ignore her. She could be very ignorant and he had no intention of getting involved in an argument just now. He reflected that she was probably upset because she hadn't seen him for a few days.

He had meant to come home the night before but, since it was Friday, he opted to spend some time at Shortie's. There he lost then won some money gambling. Then Kelly arrived with some new girls and they all went to a shebeen in South London. The music was good so they danced, smoked, and drank until the early hours. D. had gotten friendly with one of the girls who had recently arrived from Jamaica. As they talked, they discovered that they had acquaintances in common back in Kingston. She had never spoken to him before but knew of him and had seen him in her area several times. He told her that he had been in the country just over a year, and was doing some business. The girl was quite taken by him. He made a few compliments about the way she looked, bought her drinks, and made her feel comfortable. She was staying with one of Kelly's girls, so when they left, she didn't object to D. coming home with her. When he woke up, it was Saturday afternoon; he decided it was time to go home to Jenny.

Feeling a little hungry, D. went to the kitchen to prepare some lunch. For a brief moment he had contemplated asking Jenny to cook for him, but he thought better of it. It would only start her arguing. He wanted to eat, get changed, then go and look for Charlie, who had returned from New York that morning. He was frying some plantain when Jenny marched into the kitchen. She stood there for a few seconds, an angry look on her face, her stomach bulging before her.

'So wha' you ah seh, Jen?' he asked relaxed.

That seemed to make her more upset. She puffed and put her hands on her hips.

'What d'you think this is? A hotel?'

By the tone of her voice, she was ready to explode. D. tried to defuse the situation.

'Easy now, baby. You know seh I was busy this week . . . You want some lunch?'

It didn't work. Jenny was furious.

'You take me for a fool, ain't it?! You think you can disappear for days and just walk in without explanation? You know the baby is due any time now and you don't even phone to see if I'm all right . . . And where did you sleep, eh?'

D. turned over the slices of plantain in the frying pan. He was determined to keep calm.

'What kind ah question is dat?' he retorted, looking at her sideways.

'Answer me!' Jenny was shouting now. 'And don't try to tell me lies. You must think I don't know you have a woman in Hackney?'

D. put the slices of plantain on a plate and started to cut some hard dough bread, ignoring the hysterical Jenny.

'I'm not going to put up with this kind of life any more. I've had enough of the way you treat me . . . And it's gonna be worse when this baby is born . . .' She stopped for a moment, tears of anger welling up in her eyes. 'You don't care about anything, do you? I should have known better than getting involved with you . . . But I'm not going to let you wreck my life.'

D. finished buttering the bread and turned towards her. 'Cool now, man! You shouldn't get vex in your condition—'

She cut him short. 'What do you care about my condition? I'm gonna have your baby and you're running around and sleeping out.'

She began to sob heavily. He put down the carton of juice and stretched out his arm towards her shoulder. She slapped his hand away angrily and stepped back.

'Don't touch me! I don't want nothing to do with you. And I don't want your drugs in my home any more. Just get out!'

She had stopped crying and was standing by the door, her hand pointing towards the corridor. D. looked her straight in the eyes. He tried to stay calm.

'Watcha now; I don't like how you talk to me. You don't have to get mad dem way deh. Me and you talk later, seen?!'

But Jenny was too angry to listen to reason. All the frustration she had been suppressing for so long was now coming out. 'Talk? There's nothing to talk about. You're just a bastard. Get out, now! You hear me, get out!' She took a step forward and went to grab D.'s shirt.

'Easy, man! Easy . . .' he said, pushing her hand away.

But there was no stopping Jenny now. In her fury, she wanted to hurt him somehow. His unconcerned and relaxed manner was making her all the more furious.

Undeterred by the ease with which he brushed her aside, she lifted her closed fist and aimed for his face. The blow didn't connect. Instinctively, D. drew back and, as her fist whistled past him, he slapped her across the face with the back of his hand. She stumbled under the blow and, pulled down by her own weight, crashed against the kitchen wall. She slumped down and remained there, crying, a thin red line at the corner of her mouth where the knuckles had split her lip.

Alerted by the commotion, Carol appeared at the kitchen door and rushed to attend to her sister. She had elected to stay out of the argument, knowing that she shouldn't get involved in someone else's domestic dispute, but fighting was a different matter. By then, D. could feel a cold anger rising inside him. He took a last look at Jenny

124

on the floor, kissed his teeth, and walked out of the kitchen.

He went to the bedroom and rapidly gathered some of his clothes and shoes in a travel bag. He then collected a few personal belongings in the living room and headed straight out of the flat, ignoring Carol's recriminations. He had no time to waste with a girl who had no respect for him. Besides, he felt much more comfortable at Donna's house.

Downstairs, he put his bag in the boot of the car and drove out. Opening the glove compartment, he selected a cassette and pushed it into the machine. He took the spliff he had left in the ashtray and lit it. Ten minutes later, he was relaxed. He couldn't afford to let women worry him. He needed to see Charlie and take care of business.

He still felt a little hungry but that could wait. He looked in the mirror and smiled at his reflection. He would buy some food at the café on the way.

D. parked his car a little way from Charlie's house. He was taking no chances when it came to security nowadays. He had made a stop at the restaurant on the front line and eaten some food. At the nearby pub, he found Blacka shooting pool with some of his friends. Sticks and Robbie hadn't shown up yet so he left orders for them to wait for him.

Charmaine's face appeared briefly at the window after he rang the bell. She came down and opened the door.

'Hi D., you're OK?' She smiled.

'Yeah . . . Charlie deh ya?'

'He just woke up. Come.'

He followed her upstairs. She went to get Charlie

while he waited in the living room with Marcus who was busy kicking a football around. D. started to play with the child, teasing him, balancing the ball on one foot then the other, keeping it out of the little boy's reach. After a while, Marcus got so frustrated that he delivered two solid kicks to D.'s shins. D. laughed and gave the child back his ball.

'So you ah bad bwoy . . .' he said, gently poking Marcus in the stomach.

The little boy smiled, holding his football tightly in his tiny arms. D. teased him every time he came around, but Marcus was used to it and loved him all the same. Charlie came down the stairs, dressed in jogging pants and vest, wiping his face with the towel that hung around his neck.

'What's happening, D.?'

'Cool, me breddah.'

D. patted Marcus on the head and followed Charlie into the kitchen. He sat on a chair while his partner made himself a hot drink. Charlie offered him one, but he declined. They had talked on the phone a few days earlier, everything was in order. The two girls Charlie had sent back from New York had arrived the previous weekend and had been paid after delivering their packages. D. had sent one to the lab for processing while the rest had been kept by Charmaine until Charlie arrived.

'So, how New York stay?' D. asked.

Charlie sat at the table and shook his head. 'Things rough out there, man!' He took a sip from his drink then went on. 'All the youths carry pieces, heavy ones too, and they just rob and shoot each other every day. A few of my old friends got busted. Some got shot, it's a ugly scene.'

D. listened with interest to Charlie's account of life in the Big Apple.

'There's not enough territory for everybody. It's like the Wild West out there, I'm telling you.' Charlie laughed.

He finished his drink, got up, and brought out a large biscuit tin from one of the cupboards above the sink. Then from a drawer in the kitchen unit, he took out a flat, lacquered wooden box, opened it and set up the silver scales set it contained on the table. D. watched him as he carefully tipped a little of the white powder in the tin on to a formica board and proceeded to weigh up small amounts which he then transferred to small plastic bags.

'So I hear you touch Blue's t'ing . . .' Charlie remarked casually as he tipped one of the silver plates with a trickle of cocaine from a small spoon.

'How you hear 'bout dat already? D. asked, squinting.

'Come on, man, we work together. These news travel, you know . . .'

D. took a Rizla out of his pocket and peeled off a few sheets.

'Well, I've got to smoke out the bwoy . . . I want to get this business done with.'

He spread some tobacco, ganja, and a sprinkle of white powder on the paper and rolled a spliff. Charlie had weighed about a dozen small bags. The bulk of the cocaine they got from each shipment was processed into crack, but it was good business policy to keep some powder to sell, at a good price, to close associates and privileged customers. Charlie looked up from his work.

'You have to watch out for them things, star. It ain't cool to get busted for that, you know what I mean?'

D. lit the spliff and inhaled deeply. 'Don't worry 'bout it, dat's the way I operate, seen?!'

He had spoken looking straight at Charlie, with a hint of defiance in his voice. D. didn't like anyone to question, or even advise him, on what he considered to be his personal business. Charlie, on the other hand, knew that such rash action could bring some heat on his friend. It wasn't like dealing with Yard women who would never go to the police.

Seeing that it was a touchy subject, Charlie didn't press the point any further. He watched as his partner took out his knife and used the blade to draw a small amount of cocaine his way. D. deftly formed two thin lines and, bending over the table, snorted them one at a time. He then leaned back in the chair, sniffing sharply.

Charlie cleaned the scales, poured the remnant of the cocaine in the tin and put everything back in place. D. lit up the rest of his spliff and took a deep pull. Charlie reflected that his partner seemed to get more involved with the drug than he should. He had previously warned him about the dangers of overdoing it, but D. was becoming increasingly sensitive to criticism. Charlie had decided not to mention it again, but he was wondering how far this could go on before it started to affect his judgement.

Charlie knew when he started to work with D. that the man had a bad temper and was used to having his own way. But violence was bad for business and, using all his diplomacy, Charlie had so far managed to restrain him from doing anything rash. However, in the last few months he had started to see that even he no longer had any influence over D. Charlie had witnessed already, the radical changes cocaine abuse could bring to a man's personality. Some of his former friends had gone down that road of self-destruction, shunning the advice of those close to them, following only their own inner delusions until madness or death overtook them. He wondered for a brief moment how far down that path D. had reached.

'I've got some news that might interest you,' Charlie said, stretching.

D. didn't seem to have heard him. He was staring out

128

the window behind Charlie, deep in a meditation of his own. Then, as he was about to call his attention, Charlie saw his gaze alter.

'Hmmm . . . seh wha'?' D.'s voice sounded lazy.

'Fox is dead.'

D. frowned, his eyes staring deep into Charlie's as if to check whether it might be a joke. 'Dead . . .?' he repeated.

'Yeah, man,' Charlie confirmed. 'Someone called from Miami last week to talk to my spar. They said that some guys stopped by Fox's car at a traffic light, sprayed him and his bodyguard, and drove off.'

Charlie could see that D. was trying to make sense of the information.

'Who dem seh do it?' he asked after a while.

Charlie shrugged, spreading his arms outwards.

'The word is that the Spicers blame the Colombians . . . but you know how it go. It's only rumours.'

D. stayed silent for a moment. Fox was running the London operation for the outfit, there seemed to be no direct connection with someone who could have got him killed all the way down in Miami. As far as D. knew, there was no declared war with the Colombians, or even the Cubans for that matter. He looked at Charlie. 'What do you t'ink?'

Charlie shook his head. 'It's hard to say, man. Maybe he dissed someone important down there, maybe he had some old enemies.'

A thought flashed through D.'s mind but he kept it to himself. Charmaine walked into the kitchen. She looked at Charlie. 'Am I disturbing?'

'It's OK,' Charlie said.

She filled a pan with water and put it on the cooker. She lit the fire and took some vegetables out of the fridge.

'So how is Jenny?' she asked without stopping, briefly glancing at D.

There was a silence. She turned to him, wondering if he had heard the question.

'Cool, you know . . .'

The tone of his voice and the expression on his face deterred her from asking anything further. She returned to her cooking. Charlie and D. went to the living room and talked for a while about some business matters, then D. took his leave. He told Charlie to meet him at a local session later that evening, hinting that he would introduce him to some 'fresh' girls. Charlie laughed and said that he would pass. He had some moves to make first.

D. got back to his car, still feeling the strength of 'the contact' in the back of his head. He drove leisurely, music blaring out of the speakers behind him, enjoying the relaxed atmosphere of the cool Saturday evening. He considered going by Donna's for dinner but he wasn't hungry. He decided to get back to the pub to see if his soldiers had arrived. On the front line, groups of youths were hanging around, talking animatedly amongst themselves and calling out to passing cars, trying to attract prospective customers. D. slowed down to talk to a girl he knew. She didn't look over sixteen, but with her style of dress and assured manner she could have passed for much older. Leaving her to return to her friends he drove down one of the back streets and parked the car.

Inside the pub, a lively debate was in progress around the pool table. The voices of the men arguing were so loud that they almost drowned the music. D. observed Robbie as he gesticulated, intent on proving his point to another youth who was disagreeing vehemently. In the middle of a sentence Robbie turned his head and caught D.'s eyes on him across the crowded room. Handing the pool stick to the man next to him, he said a few final words to his opponent and pushed his way over to D. There was too much noise inside the pub. The two men walked out and stood outside. The setting sun was low over the row of terraced houses, bathing the whole street in a kind of golden glow that made faces shine. For the Jamaican-born amongst the youths who were talking and hustling by the roadside, evenings like these reminded them of the island they had left far behind . . . D. and Robbie leaned against a garden wall, taking in the scene.

Music pumped out of parked cars, people walked up and down by the shops and the restaurant, in and out of the pub, calling out to each other from both sides of the road. From time to time, a police van drove up the road at low speed, largely ignored by the clusters of young men and women who had made this area their stomping ground. The half-dozen officers who stared out of the windows of the vans like caged animals, were part of what was called 'high-profile' policing. They knew that the intended intimidation didn't work, yet they had to make it look like they were in control. Unless they were prepared to provoke a full-scale insurrection, there was no way they would leave the safety of the van even if they saw something outside that gave them reason to.

The roar of a powerful engine came from the top of the street towards them at full speed. D. squinted against the glare of the sun, trying to make up the car. He recognized Sticks' new green Saab before it screeched to a halt in front of them. Two pretty girls, dressed in designer sportswear and adorned with expensive jewellery, were sitting in the car. Sticks stepped out, looking sharp in a silk suit and dark glasses.

'Respect, Don,' he grinned, holding out his fist as a greeting.

'Yes, my youth!' D. said as he touched Robbie's fist with his own.

'Wait, which part you ah go flex so, man?' D. laughed.

Sticks shrugged with a modest smile. 'I jus' cruising my girls dem.'

Robbie leant against the car and started to engage the girls in a conversation.

'So, wha'ppen?' D. asked.

'I look for you earlier but dem tell me seh you come and gone already.'

Sticks dug into his pocket and pulled out a wad of banknotes bound with an elastic band. He glanced around briefly before handing it to D.

'I collect this from Willie and Longa, I don't find Stammer yet . . .' Sticks quoted the amount from each of the two dealers.

D. slipped the bundle in his pocket, mentally registering the figures. He told Sticks to stall any new supplies until the remainder of the money had been collected from everyone. Charlie wanted to check all the accounts first.

They talked for a while, leaving Robbie to chat up the girls. A grey BMW with three men inside slowed down. The driver called out to Sticks and waved, he nodded to D. before driving off.

'I know dat face . . .' D. searched his brain trying to remember.

'Yeah, man . . .' Sticks said. 'Pablo, from Red Hills Road . . . Him just come over last month. Him seh him wan' work for you.'

D. knew the man from back home. A daring youth who made a living from breaking into houses in uptown Kingston. He once got shot by a security guard and still managed to make it back to his area with three bullets inside him.

'I'll talk to him,' D. said.

'I going High Noon later,' Sticks offered. He intended to go and 'model' with his girls at the dance.

D. nodded in the direction of the car.

'You better watch dat big youth deh, him good to take dem away from you,' he grinned.

'Weh you ah seh, D.? Robbie and I ah brethren,' Sticks said dismissively, before walking to the car to check things . . . just in case. By then, Robbie was sitting in the car with the girls, who seemed quite responsive to his charm. Sticks stepped in to reclaim his property.

D. decided that he would go by Donna's to rest until he was ready to go to the dance. He told the soldiers that he would meet them there later, leaving them to negotiate over the two pretty girls. Before getting back in his car, he bought some chocolates for Cindy. He enjoyed seeing the expression on her face every time he brought her something.

Donna was sitting with two of her friends when D. arrived. He nodded to them and called out to Cindy, who was immersed in the television programme she was watching. The little girl's eyes twinkled as D. handed her the chocolates. She glanced towards her mother, but Donna smiled and said nothing.

'You're hungry?' Donna asked.

D. shook his head. He caught Donna's silent question as she saw the travel bag he was carrying. He walked down to the bedroom, leaving her to her friends. He thought he'd lie down for a moment but by the time he stretched on the bed, the lack of sleep from the previous night caught up with him and he gradually dozed off.

When he woke up, he found Donna sitting beside him

133

on the bed. He turned and rubbed a hand over his face. Everything was quiet. He glanced at his watch. It was after two in the morning. He got up and looked out of the window. He could feel Donna's eyes on him.

'Is wha'ppen?' he asked.

She smiled mysteriously and said nothing.

'Al'right, you gwan. When you ready you will tell me anyway.'

He took off his shirt and headed for the bathroom. He took a shower. When he got back to the bedroom, Donna was still sitting on the bed. D. took some clothes out of the wardrobe.

'So, you're travelling?!' Donna said, trying to sound innocent.

D. finished dressing before he answered.

'It coming like you want to know something.' He sat on the bed and put on his shoes. Looking at Donna with a sly smile, he quipped, 'I noticed how you put up my clothes dem already . . .'

The empty travel bag was neatly folded on top of the wardrobe. It was Donna's turn to be sarcastic.

'Well, maybe your girlfriend throw you out. I don't want you to sleep out ah street.'

She had spoken the word 'girlfriend' as insultingly as she could. D. threw her a cold look and she left it at that.

'You too feisty,' he said.

'You look nice,' she answered, looking him up and down admiringly.

He smiled at her. Fixing his hat in front of the mirror, he took a last look at himself then turned around.

'I'll be back later, seen?!'

Donna raised her eyebrows and watched him leave the room. D. took his mobile phone and headed out.

The night air was cool outside. Well-dressed couples

were coming out of their cars and heading for a block of flats where, judging by the loud music, a party was in full swing. D. drove out through Clapton towards Stamford Hill where the session was taking place. He was half-way there when the phone rang. It was Sticks.

'Hear dis. You best come fast. Blue ina de dance . . .'

D. was silent for a few seconds before answering. 'Don't do not'ing till I come.'

'I'm outside, by my car. I left Robbie and Blacka in deh.'

D. was about to speak when he heard Sticks swear, then the line went dead. Something was happening . . . D. felt himself go cold inside. Pressing the gas pedal to the floor, he sent the car hurtling forward at full speed, overtaking everything in front of him. He burned the lights at the crossroads and caused a few cars to swerve out of his way. The tyres of the Mercedes screamed as he sent it down the narrow street off the High Road. The dance was keeping in an old school. As he brought the car to a halt in front of the gates, he saw a crowd running out of the hall. Some women were screaming. Groups of people were crouching behind the few dozen cars parked inside the yard.

He took his gun out from underneath the dashboard and ran towards the hall, trying to see his way through the fleeing crowd. Ten yards away from the gate, he saw Sticks' car and headed towards it. The tall soldier was behind it, his eyes fixed on the entrance of the hall. His face had no expression. He held his gun at the ready. He recognized D. in time, just as he was about to point the gun at him. Blacka was sitting on the ground. The right side of his shirt looked wet.

Sticks looked straight at D. 'Blue was ina de dance with two bwoys when we got here. So I told Robbie and

Blacka to keep cool while I went to the car to call you and pick up my piece, just in case . . . As I was talking to you, I hear two shots and people started to run out.'

D. looked at Blacka, holding his shoulder. The soldier shook his head.

'After Sticks left we with the two girls, Blue was watching . . . Den one of the man dem with him started to trace we, and call we names. I told Robbie to cool, but him just answer dem. Next t'ing I know, Robbie walk towards dem, so I go fe stop him . . . As I reach him, Blue pull out a gun and fire one shot in the air, so the people started to scatter and him just shot Robbie ina de chest. People was running everywhere, den the same man who was ah diss we, come right up to me and stab me. I never see him come t'rough the crowd. I jus' hit him with a bottle and run . . .'

D. said nothing. He could see the entrance now. There was now only a trickle of people hurrying out. He peeled his eyes as he recognized a tall silhouette amongst a group of screaming women. Blue and two others were walking fast towards the outside gates, about thirty yards away. D. pointed them out to Sticks. They crouched behind the car, guns trained on the three men above the bonnet, and waited until they were in a straight line. Simultaneously, D. and Sticks opened fire. D. saw the soldier who was closing the way fall down. Recovering from the surprise, Blue aimed towards the car and fired three shots, then he and the other soldier started running. They turned left at the gates.

'Go and check Robbie!' D. shouted to Blacka, as he and Sticks took off after their targets.

As they reached the gates, they saw a black Volvo speeding away towards the top of the road. D. ran to his car, started the engine and did a U-turn in the narrow street, barely missing a lamp post. Sticks had jumped in beside him and was inserting a new ammunition clip in his gun. D. showed him the hidden compartment under the dashboard and gave him his own gun to reload. They had turned at full speed on to the High Road. The Volvo had about three hundred yards on them, heading straight towards Tottenham. D. knew that his car would catch up with them and they must have guessed it too as they took a left and then a succession of small back streets, hoping to shake off the Mercedes.

D. was fifty yards behind the Volvo now, doing eighty miles an hour in a dark, narrow road. Meanwhile, Sticks was trying to take advantage of the straight line to shoot. He let out two bullets in rapid succession. One went wild but the second one shattered the rear screen. They saw the Volvo swerve, then turn abruptly to the left into a sloping street.

'Dem going down to the Farm,' Sticks said.

Following hard behind the Volvo, they drove into the sprawling estate. The roar of the powerful engines had filled the still night. The Volvo was only about fifty yards in front, speeding down the driveways around the flats. They went through a parking lot, swerving madly around thick concrete pillars, then the Volvo suddenly left the road and climbed onto one of the large grass verges. D. had to brake and manoeuvre to follow them across the lawn, losing a few seconds. He saw the black car steer wildly and turn behind a block of flats. Swearing, he pressed on the gas and gave chase. He screeched into the turn.

D. braked hard to avoid hitting the Volvo that stood there, front doors open and its engine and lights still on. Cautiously, D. and Sticks got out of the Mercedes and looked inside the Volvo. It was empty. D. switched off the engine and took the keys. To the left was the entrance to the basement of the flats. They walked into the darkness, slowly, guns ready to shoot. They took the stairs leading upwards, listening for any footsteps coming from above. There was only silence.

The two men reached the ground floor. Two long, dimly lit corridors led to the flats on either side of the hall. They stood still for a while, listening out. Opposite the main door, the stairway continued towards the upper floors. D. and Sticks looked at each other, both wondering whether the two fugitives had kept running upstairs or chosen the way out through the main doors. D. reflected that if one of them went upstairs and the other was still somewhere on the ground floor, they could be caught in a crossfire. Besides a shootout in the flats would only result in attracting the police, and there was nothing to be gained from that. Motioning to Sticks to follow him, D. went back down the stairs leading to the basement.

'Come . . . I have a plan,' he whispered to his soldier.

They got back outside. While Sticks kept watch, D. took the key he had taken from the Volvo out of his pocket and switched the engine and the lights back on. He then went to the rear of the car, took out his knife, and punctured the two rear tyres. Handing the keys of his own car to Sticks, he told him: 'I wait here fe dem . . . Drive the car out fast, like we leaving. Just park on the road near the entrance, lights out. Dem cyan go too far with flat tyres . . .'

Confident that his strategy would work, D. went to hide behind a row of cars in the parking lot facing the flats. Sticks, meanwhile, followed his instructions and drove the Mercedes out of the estate at speed. Twenty yards away from the Volvo, his gun in hand, D. hid behind a car. It was a moonless night and the few scattered lamp posts around the flats did little to disperse the darkness. It did cross D.'s mind for a moment that Blue and his soldier might decide to leave the car and make their way out on foot through the main door of the flats. He quickly dismissed the idea as unlikely. Anyway Sticks would see them as soon as they got to the street.

Ten minutes passed. Wherever they were hiding, the two fugitives must have heard the sound of the car leaving. No matter how suspicious they were, they couldn't possibly stay inside the flats much longer. D. looked at his watch. Twenty past three . . . He took a deep breath and rubbed the back of his neck. This waiting was making him nervous. He thought of joining Sticks in the car where they would still be able to monitor anyone coming out of the estate.

D. was about to stand up when he thought he heard some sounds coming from the darkness of the basement. He stayed low behind the car, very still. Slowly a silhouette emerged from the shadows, one hand pointing outwards, carefully looking around. A few seconds later, another form, this one taller, emerged. Blue walked around his car, watchful, his weapon aimed straight in front of him at the silent night. As he passed directly in his sight, D. resisted the temptation to shoot him there and then. Blue got into the driving seat. After a last look around, his companion got into the car, the doors slammed and the Volvo reversed rapidly before turning right at the corner of the block of flats.

D. sprang out from his hiding place, ran towards the basement and up the stairs to the ground floor of the flats. He crossed the hall and reached the door just in time to see the Volvo drive around a stretch of lawn and head for the uphill ramp leading out of the estate. In his haste to get away, Blue hadn't yet noticed the flat tyres. Hoping Sticks would act quickly enough, D. opened the door and ran out after the car.

Meanwhile, from the Mercedes which he had parked strategically at the corner of the road slightly above the estate, Sticks had seen the Volvo as it drove around the flats. D.'s plan had worked. Smiling viciously, he switched on the engine but left the lights off. The gun was beside him on the passenger seat. Through the windscreen, Sticks noticed a shadow running across the lawn, behind the speeding car. The timing had to be perfect. They had to exploit the element of surprise so that Blue and his soldier had no time to react. D. was catching up with the Volvo now, as it slowed down to negotiate the ramps of the narrow driveway leading out of the estate. Sticks waited until the big car was almost at the end of the driveway. He put the Mercedes in gear, drove forward to the bend then turned sharply to the left in the path of the oncoming Volvo, switching the lights on full beam. The Volvo braked violently as Blue, blinded by the powerful lights, tried to swerve to the left. The front wheels of the Volvo climbed the concrete kerb and the car stopped there, half-way on the grass verge.

Meanwhile, Sticks had stopped the car and jumped out. A shot rang out of the driver's window and he ducked out of the way. As Blue opened the door to run out, D. sprang from behind and hit him on the back of the head with his gun butt. Blue caught on to the door of the car as he dropped forward, still holding his gun. D. stuck his barrel right against the side of Blue's throat and took the weapon from him. Meanwhile, Sticks had moved forward to the other side of the Volvo, his gun trained on the passenger seat. Cautiously, he walked up to the window and looked inside the car. The soldier was slumped forward, unconscious. He had hit his head against the dashboard in the crash. There was blood running from his open mouth.

D. stood Blue against the side of the car. The tall man was still shaken by the blow he had received. D. looked at him with cold eyes, he felt like killing him slowly, but there was no time for that. Someone in the nearby houses had certainly heard the shot and might have called the police. Still holding Blue by the collar, D. slipped his gun inside his waist. His hand went to his back pocket. He took out his knife, flashing it open with a sharp jerk of the wrist. He looked straight into his enemy's eyes . . .

'Your breddah dead already, but dis is for Jerry . . .'

Quickly, D. plunged his blade into Blue's chest. The tall man made a brief sound and tried desperately to push him away. But D. had him pinned against the car. He drew out the knife and stabbed him again in the left side. This time, Blue collapsed slowly as D. drew out the blade and stepped back. He had a last look at the tall figure now lying on its side on the ground and walked to the Mercedes. Sticks was already in the driving seat, he had reversed the car, ready to go. D. got in beside him, closed his door and they drove out. The engine of the black Volvo was still running . . .

harlie put the phone down. He stood still for a moment, absentmindedly staring at the framed map of Africa on the living-room wall. He couldn't help feeling disturbed by the recent events around him. Too much was happening, too fast . . .

Their lab had been raided by the police the previous day. A dozen officers had somehow located the flat, cut through the protective railings, smashed the door, and seized over half a pound of cocaine, plus a quantity of crack ready for distribution. Scotty, one of the chemists, who was asleep in the bedroom, was also arrested. He was likely to receive a heavy sentence, especially if he refused to name the others involved, as Charlie was sure he would. The raid was a major blow. The financial loss was great, but considering they had operated successfully for over a year without problems, apart from Sherryl's accident, there was no cause for complaint. What Charlie couldn't figure out was how the police had found the lab despite the strict security measures he had set up. Only Indian and Sticks ever went to the lab, either to deliver or collect, and they both had strict instructions on checking for eventual tails, by using alternating routes and different vehicles. Scotty and Pipe, the other chemist, took turns to occupy the flat and had the best reasons to be careful. Charlie sighed, shaking his head. He felt certain someone had informed on them. He was going to make it his priority to find out who.

The sound of the street door opening and closing brought him out of his meditation. Charmaine came up the stairs, her clothes dripping with rain. A storm had broken out during the night and the downpour had continued throughout the morning. Noticing the frown on Charlie's face, Charmaine asked, 'What's the matter?'

'I'm OK . . . just a few things to take care of.'

Charmaine had learned not to ask questions about her man's business. From time to time she overheard bits of conversation and managed to form a vague idea of what was happening, but it served no purpose to try to find out too much. As long as Charlie was safe, that was all that mattered.

'I've been to see Jenny . . .' she said, taking off her wet jacket.

Charlie remembered her mentioning something about that as she had left him in bed early that morning. Jenny had been taken to hospital the previous evening, her labour pains having started. Charlie went to the window and briefly looked at the grey sky outside before sitting on the sofa. He had started to watch a movie earlier but had missed most of it while making phone calls. Charmaine took off her shoes and came to sit beside him.

'She will probably have the baby sometime today . . . I'm going back later.' She tried to draw Charlie's attention.

'How is she?' His eyes were on the screen.

'She's in pain, but the doctor said everything's fine.' Charmaine paused, then: 'She asked for D. . . .'

Charlie made a kind of mumbling sound. He knew what was coming next. There was a silence as Charmaine thought of the best way to formulate her request. She spoke cautiously. 'If you told him, would he go and see her?'

Charlie smiled despite the grim thoughts occupying

his mind. He turned towards Charmaine. She had a sly way of putting things to him which she knew he wouldn't like. She would adopt an innocent face, fix him with her long, dark eyes and ask seemingly non-pressuring questions until, through politely veiled hints, she gently cornered him into agreeing to whatever request she had.

'So you want me to ask D. to go to the hospital?' Charlie decided to cut the game short.

She raised her eyebrows and nodded.

'D. don't listen to no one nowadays,' Charlie said.

'Jenny's in pain, you know . . . It would mean a lot to her.'

'Look, baby, I'll mention it to him, but I'll be surprised if he goes.'

Charmaine frowned, trying to contain her feminine indignation. 'I know they had a quarrel, but she's having his baby . . .'

Charlie laughed. 'That don't mean nothing to D., you know what I mean?'

Charmaine was silent for a while. Charlie tried to give her the impression he was watching the movie but he knew she was unlikely to stop there. She didn't.

'What's the matter with him?' she asked finally. 'He's just rough, like he hasn't got no feelings . . . I mean, you're not like that . . .'

Charlie looked at his woman, straightfaced. He was unwilling to discuss D.'s attitude to life or people. There were many things Charmaine just wouldn't understand. She read the message on his face and asked nothing more. They watched television in silence until Marcus woke up and called his mother from his upstairs bedroom.

*

Over the din of the music, Sticks heard two large knocks on the door. He came out of the kitchen and glanced briefly through the peephole before opening the door for D.

'Wha' ah gwan?'

'Cool . . . Everybody reach except Linton.'

Sticks locked the door behind them and said, 'I bring a youth called Slinga fe see you.'

D. looked at the tall soldier waiting for him to explain.

'Him seh him know who inform about the lab . . . him don't wan' fe talk to no one but the don,' Sticks said.

D. nodded, pleased by the information. Sticks went back into the kitchen. D. followed the corridor and turned right into the living room. The music was deafeningly loud. Everyone interrupted their conversations to greet him as he entered. He crossed the room and sat down next to Charlie. They had called a meeting of all the members of the team following the raid on the lab. Meanwhile, everyone had been ordered to keep a low profile and wait for new instructions. Charlie wanted to find out just how serious the situation was. Had the raid only been the result of a lucky break for the police or did they know about the whole operation?

D. built himself a cocktail spliff and looked around the room. Busy talking and smoking were Blacka, Indian, and Pipe the chemist. Also present was Pablo, brought in on Sticks' recommendation as a possible replacement for Robbie. A short, dark youth with deep-set eyes was sitting in the far corner, watching the television with a blank expression. D. assumed that he was Slinga, the youth Sticks had mentioned. He couldn't remember ever having seen him before. Judging by his ordinary clothes and the absence of jewellery, he was probably newly arrived. The fact that he had insisted on delivering his information personally indicated that he was probably looking for a job with the outfit. D. lit his spliff.

The music stopped abruptly as the cassette ended. Sticks walked into the room and went to turn it over. On his way back out, he stopped by Slinga and whispered a few words to him. A few minutes later, the youth got up and walked around the back of the sofa to where D. was sitting. Squatting beside the chair, he leaned slightly forward.

'Respect, Don.' Slinga's voice was deep, the voice of a man older than he was.

D. took a draw from the spliff. 'You have somet'ing fe me, star?'

Speaking close to D.'s ear against the loud music, Slinga divulged his information. He explained that he had been taken to the police station about a week earlier regarding a 'little problem'. While he was being questioned by an officer, another policeman had walked into the interrogation room and said something to his colleague about having a man prepared to give information concerning a lab. Slinga realized that the informer was in the next room and, a little later, managed to have a brief look at the man. It was only a few days after this, when he heard about the raid, that Slinga made the connection and decided to talk to D. After listening to the youth, D. turned to face him.

'You know who the boy is?'

'I check out 'pon him. Some junkie named Barry . . . live local.'

Slinga had done some nice work. D. looked into the deep, dark eyes. Slinga stood the stare.

'Which part you from, star?' D. asked.

'Nannyville.'

'Is when you come over?'

'About three months now.'

Linton and Sticks walked into the room.

'Al'right youth, check me when the meeting done, seen?!'

The youth got up and walked back to his seat. D. was sure he wasn't over sixteen years of age, yet there was something much older in the steely eyes and the quiet, self-assured demeanour. Leaving the matter to rest until later, D. concentrated on the meeting at hand. Sticks turned down the music and they got down to business. Charlie started by summing up the situation and explained that they would need a new base to process crack from. He mentioned the arrest of Scotty, stressing that their business was a risky one where everyone needed to operate under strict security. Blacka and Linton, who had been sent to scout around for premises, reported that they had identified a few places which might be suitable for a new lab. Charlie gave instructions to inform the dealers that everything would proceed as usual. They all knew about the raid and it was vital to reassure them that they wouldn't run short of supplies.

The meeting went on for a couple of hours, all the participants helping themselves to the bottles of beer and soft drinks provided. Once the important business had been taken care of, Pablo was introduced to the team as Robbie's replacement. Robbie was still in intensive care under police guard. Nothing was said about Slinga, but since he was at the meeting, everyone assumed he was also a new member.

D. had discreetly called Charlie aside and told him about Slinga. Charlie was impressed. He asked D. whether the boy wanted a job as a chemist, since they needed someone to replace Scotty. D. said he would decide that after he had talked to the youth some more.

'What we're going to do about the informer?' Charlie asked.

D. looked at him, squinting. 'Make the new soldiers dem do the job . . .'

Charlie nodded thoughtfully, looking at Pablo, then Slinga in turn. The rest of the team were getting busy burning crack and drinking, the music was back on at high volume. The atmosphere in the room was soon totally relaxed. The coke pipes had been circulating and it showed on their faces. D. looked at Slinga sipping from a bottle of beer. The youngster had warmed up to the others and was now listening attentively to Indian who seemed to be explaining something important to him. After a while, Slinga became aware of D.'s stare and turned sharply towards him. Answering D.'s subtle call, he excused himself to Indian and came over. D. took a sip from his drink.

'Hear me now; I appreciate wha' you do fe we, star. So I gwan set you up, seen?! You can get some pounds, or some business to hustle so you can make a raise. Weh you ah seh?'

Slinga's face showed no expression. He looked away, as if considering the offer. Then he faced D., pausing for a few seconds before answering.

'Don, mek I show you somet'ing; the reason I come fe tell you about the informer is because I don't like fe see no bwoy try mash up a man business. The whole a we a Yard man, and when we reach ah foreign we ha fe stick together. But I don't wan' de man feel like ouno ah owe me somet'ing, seen?! I don't do it fe money . . . Dat ah no not'ing.'

Slinga stopped and looked down briefly. D. could see he had something more to say. There was a silence then he said, 'Still, me nah tell you no lie, Don; me is a youth just come over and I check out the scene, observe how t'ings

148

operate ah Inglan . . . Right now it's progress me ah deal wid, and I know you is de best man fe work for. I can do anyt'ing, you know, Don . . . Any kind ah work, I can do it.'

D. had tested Slinga, checked his character. He could now see that the youth wasn't just after a quick raise. He had ambition and sounded positive. D. smiled.

'It look like you have a good heart. I need a man like you ina de team.' D. paused, then, 'I have one job to be done, but since you is new to de team, I don't know if you can take care ah dat . . .'

Slinga passed his hand over his short cropped hair, before answering: 'Anyt'ing dat needs to be done, I will handle it.'

D. took another sip from his bottle. Looking straight into Slinga's eyes he said slowly: 'Dat informer bwoy hurt de business, him must pay de price . . .'

Slinga stood the stare. After listening, he grinned slightly for the first time. 'No problem,' he said simply.

Donna got in the car and closed the door. The Mercedes smoothly circled the lawn and headed towards the exit. D. adjusted the volume of the stereo and lit his spliff. They were on their way to South London to pick Cindy up. She had spent some days with her cousins, Leroy's daughters. The morning was bright, despite a blanket of grey clouds looming on the horizon. D. felt relaxed. He had rested for a few days, away from the hustling scene and the night ravings.

Most of the previous week's problems had been solved. A new lab had been set up in a flat near where Sticks lived, which made security a little easier. Trading had resumed and Charlie was organizing another shipment from the US. Things were back to normal. By all accounts, the raid had only been an isolated stroke by the police, acting on information . . . That loose end had been taken care of too. Pablo and Slinga were given the contract on the informer and a few days later Barry was found dead inside a large metal dustbin by the caretaker of a local estate. After spending two weeks in a coma, Robbie had survived the shooting and been released from hospital. However, the police had checked his immigration status and were now about to have him deported. Slinga had taken up the position of chemist to replace Scotty, who had been sentenced to five years in jail. Charlie had made sure his family was taken care of and that he wanted for nothing while serving his time.

Driving on the High Street, D. kept checking his mirror. Ever vigilant, he had noticed a brown car leaving the estate just behind them. He didn't think anything of it at first until fifteen minutes later he saw the same vehicle stop right behind him at the traffic lights. Calmly, D. finished his spliff and threw the butt out of the window. Donna said something to him, he answered her absent-mindedly. As the light changed to amber, D. slid the gear handle all the way down and pressed the gas pedal right down to the floor. The tyres screamed as the big car jumped forward, leaving the other vehicles twenty yards behind. Swinging the steering-wheel with both hands, he sent the Mercedes into a sharp left turn and sped down the narrow street. As he reached the crossing at the other end, D. saw the brown car taking the turn, trying to catch up with him. He looked left and right and drove across the intersection, accelerating down the street opposite.

Donna, who had kept quiet up until then, turned to him. 'Wha' happ'n to you?'

'Somebody ah follow me . . .' D. said in a flat tone of voice.

Donna looked in the side mirror. The brown car was about fifty yards behind them, getting closer as D. had to slow down to pass a van coming from the opposite direction. She frowned. 'Some white man ina de car. Could be police, you know . . .'

D. didn't answer. He turned right at the end of the road, then left into a downhill street, and took off at speed. Donna looked in the mirror and saw the car coming down after them from the top of the hill.

'It's a Rover. Must be the police!' she said, looking at D.

He could see three men inside the car.

He felt a cold anger rise inside him. He didn't like to be chased and running away wasn't his style, even from the police. Frowning, he hooked a forceful right turn, then right again. While driving at speed, he pushed his left hand far under the dashboard and brought out his cloth-wrapped gun. Donna saw the move and turned sharply towards him, her eyes wide open in disbelief as he took out the weapon and unlocked the safety mechanism.

'Wha' you ah do, man . . .?!' There was fear in her voice.

D. gave her a brief look. She saw the frozen half-squint, the slight contraction pinching the left corner of his mouth. She called out again with urgency. 'D.! Listen to me, man. You cyan shoot police! You hear me?'

He said nothing. The Rover was only yards behind them now, horn blowing, lights flashing for him to stop. He could hear Donna pleading with him, fear exuding from her, but something in his head was urging him to trap the pursuing policemen and riddle their car with

151

bullets. Donna's hand was on his hand now, holding it down and squeezing. When she spoke again, her voice was a whisper.

'D., I beg you listen to me . . . Dem deh police carry gun too. Anyhow you shoot after dem, dem will have a excuse fe kill you. Please, let it go . . . Dem cyan do you not'ing.'

Slowly, she managed to loosen his grip on the gun. She held his hand while she took the weapon, sliding it into her waist, under her blouse. D. was still driving at speed. Staring right ahead. Donna wiped small beads of sweat from her forehead with the back of her hand and looked anxiously in the side mirror. The driver of the Rover was doing his best to overtake him but there just wasn't enough space.

As calmly as she could, Donna said: 'Gimme anything else you have, before you stop . . .'

D. inhaled deeply and glanced at her briefly. He pushed his hand under the dashboard once more and handed her an ammunition clip for the gun. Donna took it swiftly and hid it in her clothing. The horn of the Rover was blowing loudly, right behind them. Passers-by stopped as they passed, looking curiously at the two speeding cars.

'It's al'right, you can stop now . . .' Donna said.

D. drove another hundred yards before slowing down and finally stopping. There was the screeching of brakes behind them, then the loud crack of doors violently opened.

Two white men dressed in jeans and leather jackets rushed to the Mercedes, while the third one stood by the Rover watching.

'Out of the car! Now!' One of the policemen shouted

to D., pulling open the door of the car. D. stepped out calmly and looked at the officer as he quickly flashed his badge.

'What you want with me?' he asked.

'Why didn't you stop when we signalled you?'

D. smiled. 'I have to be careful, you know. You could have been some gangsters . . .'

The policeman didn't appreciate the joke. 'What's your name?' he barked.

D. gave him his assumed identity.

'You have any papers on you?'

'My licence is in the glove compartment,' D. said relaxed.

The policeman signalled to his colleague on the other side of the car to check inside. Donna was standing by, looking bewildered. She had managed to convince the officer who was questioning her that she had no idea of what was happening and had asked D. to stop and find out what was wrong. The second policeman handed D.'s licence to his colleague over the roof of the car. The officer looked at it.

'We have some questions to ask you, you have to follow us to the station,' he said coldly.

D. looked at him with a puzzled expression. 'What questions? I haven't done anyt'ing wrong.'

The policeman insisted. 'Are you coming willingly?'

By the tone of his voice, D. knew that the officer only needed half an excuse to rough him up. He breathed deeply then, grinning at the straight-faced officer, he nodded with resignation.

'OK, I'll come with you. What about my car?'

'We'll take care of it,' the other policeman said.

D. shrugged, shook his head and started to walk

153

towards the Rover, closely followed by the officer. Before getting in the back of the police car, he called out to Donna looking deeply into her eyes.

'Call a lawyer fe me, seen?!'

Donna nodded silently. 'Where you taking him?' she asked the second officer.

'Stoke Newington, miss,' he answered as he got into the Mercedes. He put it into gear and drove off followed by his colleagues in the Rover.

Donna stood there looking, as the two cars turned the corner and disappeared from sight. She remained still on the pavement for a short while, just staring ahead, oblivious to the few people who had stopped to observe the scene. Deep inside her the tension subsided and she started walking. Almost mechanically, she placed her left hand against her waist and felt the sharp edges of the gun beneath the soft garment. She forced herself to relax and turned right into another street, away from the curious stares she could still feel behind her.

She was afraid for D. but reassured herself, thinking that, had she not succeeded in restraining him, this could have been the last morning of their lives. She took a deep breath and straightened her thoughts. She needed to get to a phone, fast.

D. was in the police station until late afternoon. After being searched, he was locked up in a cell in the basement of the building and left there for a few hours, presumably to soften him up for the interrogation. Having experienced detention in Jamaica, D. found the small room quite comfortable in comparison and settled quietly on the bunk. He reflected on his situation for a while and realized that the police were unlikely to have any evidence for whatever they suspected him of doing. If they had, they would have charged him right away. All the same, he didn't enjoy being locked up. He thought about Donna and smiled. If it hadn't been for her keeping her head, he would probably be in serious trouble by now . . . Donna had probably contacted Charlie first, he would know where to get a lawyer.

D. was absorbed in his thoughts, almost dozing, when he heard footsteps stop in front of his cell, followed by the sound of a key turning in the lock. A uniformed policeman opened the heavy door and told him he was wanted upstairs. D. was led along a corridor to a room where the two plainclothes officers who had arrested him were sitting at a large table. They watched attentively as he sat on the chair opposite them.

The youngest of the two, with short cropped hair and a thin moustache, pressed the touch buttons of a small recorder placed on the table in front of him. The other officer, the one who had first talked to D. when they had stopped him, was a tall, middle-aged man with piercing blue eyes. He asked D. his name and address. D. answered the question, and the ones that followed, effortlessly composed, sticking to his assumed identity.

The interview went smoothly enough. The two policemen wanted to know about his possible connections to Blue's killing, the crack lab that they raided, and the death of Barry the informer. D. stayed calm and told them that, although he heard about all this on the street, they had nothing to do with him. He could see that the policemen didn't believe him, but they had nothing to disprove his claim, and they knew that he knew it. Seeing that they were not getting anywhere, the older officer tried to regain the advantage by enquiring as to how D. could afford the car he was driving, suggesting that he had to be involved in some kind of trafficking or other illegal activity. D. smiled, only just refraining from telling the policeman that he was probably jealous of him. The police didn't like to see a black man driving an expensive car. Envy certainly played a part in their enquiries. Relaxed, D. explained that he was a producer and promoter in the music business, setting up shows and various event. That was how he earned a living. Besides, he pointed out to the two frustrated policemen, the car was on hire-purchase in his girlfriend's name . . .

D. was in the interrogating room about an hour when there was a knock on the door. A young uniformed policewoman opened the door and stuck her head in the room to inform the officers that D.'s lawyer had finally arrived. On the instruction of the older detective, she brought in a neatly dressed burly man with glasses and well-combed grey hair. He introduced himself, enquired whether D. was all right, and announced politely but firmly that unless his client was being formally charged, he would have to be released. The officers seemed annoyed but had no option but to comply with the request. The older one made a point of telling D. that they would see him again . . . D. didn't answer. His only concern was staying out of reach for now.

After collecting his belongings from the desk, he asked for his car which, he was told, was parked outside. Once outside the station, he stopped briefly to talk to the lawyer who advised him to be careful, as the police were unlikely to leave the matter unresolved. D. thanked him and told him to send the bill for his services to his address. The Mercedes was across the street. He walked up to it, opened the door and got inside. He knew the car had been searched, but the police hadn't found anything, else they wouldn't have let him go so easily. He turned on the stereo and drove out, thanking his luck for being back outside in the mellow sunset.

The restless crowd was spreading beyond the barriers erected to keep it in order, spilling over into the street like a colourful and vibrant procession. On the road, the traffic had come to a virtual standstill. There were no more parking spaces available anywhere around the West London venue where the annual Reggae Awards show was taking place that night. Amidst the blaring of horns, loud music from the car stereos, and the shouts of frustrated drivers heckling each other, the unfortunate residents of the nearby terraced houses were unlikely to get any sleep. Even the efforts of half a dozen police officers weren't enough to ease the congestion. Behind the large glass entrance doors of the venue, beefy bouncers were trying to keep everything under control, letting people in two at a time and searching them for concealed weapons. A few hundred revellers had already been admitted and about as many were stretching out in a formless queue outside. The promoters had good reasons to feel satisfied with the attendance of the event.

Through the lounge, past the cloakrooms, and several stalls where various T-shirts, badges and other items were on offer, was the hall itself. The huge room was filled with tables, large ones in the middle, smaller ones at the sides, adorned with white tablecloths and candles, some with champagne buckets already awaiting the guests. From the high ceiling antique-looking chandeliers hung and heavy velvet drapes formed the stage background. Scores of people had already settled on the balcony overlooking the hall, where rows of small tables were lined up on ascending step-platforms. The whole scene was impressive.

Reggae music blowing through the public address system stacked high at both ends of the stage greeted the incoming crowd. Women in glittering outfits and sharply dressed young men were making their way along the aisles with calculated nonchalance. Everyone was a star tonight, displaying the result of several hours and considerable sums of money spent choosing and buying their clothes to the admiring glances of others. The Reggae Awards show was one of the highlights of the social calendar. You had to be there, and to look your best. The atmosphere was electric but relaxed.

Around one of the larger tables, sipping champagne with the assured look of people accustomed to the high life, sat D. and his team. Besides Donna, whom he had brought along for this special occasion, Charmaine was the only other woman in the group. She sat in her chair throwing glances around the room at the other tables, trying to recognize anyone she might know. Next to her, Charlie was leaning back, observing with studied indifference the constant stream of new arrivals. Sticks was there, defiant-looking as usual, with a heavy gold 'cargo' hanging from his neck. To his right, Indian drew calmly on a cigarette, from time to time speaking a few words to Slinga who sat beside him, impassive as ever. Blacka was the last one of the group, dressed in a suit and tie, complete with Beaver hat and dark glasses. D. and Charlie wore similar types of two-piece, two-tone silk suits, with chinese collars and epaulettes. They both wore heavy-looking thick gold chains and medallions. To anyone who saw them, posing in their expensive clothes and jewellery, seated in front of the four champagne buckets on the table, it was obvious that D. and his team were high in the established hierarchy of the ghetto.

It took almost two more hours before everybody finally made their way into the hall and were seated. By the time the compere for the evening walked on stage, the audience was already warm and not prepared to wait any longer for the show to start. The names of some favourite artists were already being called amongst the crowd. After a few jokes, most of which fell flat, the compere realized that the audience were in no mood for any more delay and decided to get things rolling. From behind the curtains came the roll of a drum and, suddenly, the first few bars of a hit song came crashing through the loudspeakers. The crowd went wild, cheering and calling for the band to 'rewind'. All at the same time, the compere shouted out the name of the artist whose hit tune had triggered the uproar and the drapes parted to reveal the band as it started the song from the start once more.

The audience didn't need encouraging. The name of the artist was all over the hall, called by hundreds of excited voices. When he finally came on stage, such was the din from the crowd that the song had to be taken from the top twice more. After greeting everyone and sending a few dedications, the singer was finally able to do his first number. He sang two more songs, to the general delight, before leaving the spot to the smiling compere who managed to get a round of applause for the promoters, send a few messages, and announce the next artist, in record time.

Many of the performers had flown in from Jamaica especially for the Awards show and gave their best that night, responding to the feeling from the crowd. The most popular acts – the ladies' favourites – got ecstatic receptions from their fans and obliged by inviting a few of them on stage to dance with them to their more romantic numbers. By the time the compere, who was looking increasingly taken over by the general excitement, reappeared to announce a mid-show break of half an hour, most of the audience had left their seats and were rocking as one.

At D.'s table, the champagne bottles stood empty and everyone was relaxed. Even the usually unsmiling Slinga had a grin on his face. Sticks, who had been watching a pretty young girl sitting at a nearby table, got up and swaggered over to get acquainted. From behind his shades, Blacka watched the outcome of Sticks' excursion with interest. As Charmaine got up to go to the bathroom, D. motioned over to Donna: 'Go with her!'

Donna, who had only exchanged a few words with Charmaine, rose from her chair. Charmaine stood there for a few moments waiting. She had nothing against Donna, but being Jenny's friend, she had so far refrained from socializing. She got up after Donna and followed her. D. caught Charlie's interrogative glance and smiled. He decided it was time for a smoke. Charlie declined but asked him to order more champagne. D. sent Slinga to call Sticks who by now was sitting comfortably near his girl. The three then headed for the men's washroom across the hall. They had to push their way in. The small room was filled with smoke.

Inside the washroom itself, only two men were actually using the toilets. About a dozen others were busy building spliffs or smoking. Two youths, dressed in expensive-looking suits, had loaded a small glass pipe with a piece of rock and were busy engulfing the surrounding space in thick clouds of whitish smoke. D. answered the greetings from a few of the men whom he knew. From the opposite corner of the room, a nervous looking youth with alert eyes called out to him.

'Don! Set me up now . . .'

He was wearing a suit on top of a string vest, no shirt.

160

Several gold chains hung from his neck, partly hiding the long, thin scar, lighter in tone than his dark skin, that ran from below his left ear to his chest. D. gave him a blank look. He didn't recognize the face and furthermore he wasn't into retailing, as everyone in the business knew. However, since he was in a good mood, he refrained from scolding the youth. Turning to Sticks he said, 'See wha' de bwoy want . . . and tell him don't ever make dat mistake again.'

Sticks called the youth over while D. walked to a group of three men drawing from long cone-shaped spliffs. Judging by their half-closed eyelids, it wasn't their first smoke of the evening.

'Respect, D.,' a tall, bearded man with a shaven skull said between two pulls.

'Alvin! I know seh if you ina de place, ah ya so I mus' find you,' D. laughed.

He took out some paper and started to stick some sheets together. Slinga and Sticks, who had attended to the youth after admonishing him for his impertinence, did the same. They stayed in the washroom for a while, smoking and commenting on the show with Alvin and his friends, until they heard the music in the hall fade away and the booming voice of the compere filter through the closed door. D. and his two soldiers made their way out, followed by most of the others. In the hall, people were taking their seats for the second part of the show. As they passed the bar, D. sent Slinga to order four more bottles of champagne.

Sticks led the way back to their table, but stopped suddenly. Out of the crowd massed against the back wall, two men had stepped in his path and were standing there, arms folded. Sticks was about a yard away from the nearest one, a stocky man with a thin moustache. He was wearing a red silk suit and a white fluffy Kangol hat that leaned forwards on a pair of dark sunglasses. His companion was taller and stood a little behind in a black suit, white shirt and black tie. Sticks had inconspicuously folded his hands behind his back. Looking straight at the first man, he asked: 'Is what ouno want?'

From behind his shades, the first man's gaze was fixed on D. Yet, when he spoke, the message was addressed to Sticks.

'Someone is inviting your boss for a drink upstairs . . .'

The voice was deep, the Jamaican accent tinged with unmistakable American intonations. D. took a step forward. He looked at the two men briefly, squinting. He didn't need to ask who had sent them. In a way he had been expecting the meeting for some time. Turning to Slinga he said, 'Go back to the table, tell Charlie I soon come.'

The soldier nodded and left. D. then motioned to the man in the white hat.

'Let's go!'

Sticks close behind him, he followed the two men as they made their way through the crowd to the stairs leading up to the balcony. Upstairs, they walked alongside the row of tables overlooking the hall. D. recognized Chin from the back before reaching the table. A woman was sitting facing him, dark skinned with short flat-pressed hair and heavy make-up. She looked up at D. as he stopped. He called out: 'How you do, Mr Chin?'

'Yes, D.! What's happening?'

He seemed relaxed in his white suit and bow tie. Casting a glance over D.'s outfit he grinned, nodding approvingly. 'You're looking fine, man!'

Chin turned to the woman sitting at his table. 'I need to talk to my friend here, I'll soon be back.'

He got up and nodded to his soldiers. The one with

his shades took his seat while the other one stood behind him.

'Let's take a walk somewhere more quiet,' Chin said.

Sticks had taken position on the other side of the table, behind the woman. She had turned her attention to the show, apparently unwilling to talk to the soldier facing her. D. followed Chin up the gangway and out through to the corridor where a few people were hanging out. Chin leaned against one of the carpeted pillars and looked at D.

'So, how is business?'

'Fine, you know. Everything cool.'

Chin took a pack of cigarettes out of his pocket and lit one. 'I hear you finally met with Blue . . .' he said, blowing smoke.

D. scratched the back of his head. He knew Chin wanted to talk about something in particular, but he was taking his time to get to the point.

'Yeah, I met him . . .' he answered evasively.

Chin grinned and shook his head. 'I guess he was just unlucky.' He drew from his cigarette then said casually: 'I hope you didn't lose too much in that raid recently . . .'

D. shrugged and answered, 'It's a risky business.'

Chin laughed. He paused for a moment then: 'You know, I like how you handle yourself. You're a – ' he searched for the word ' – survivor.'

D. smiled modestly. 'I do my best.'

Before Chin could continue, D. decided to take the advantage. Grinning, he said: 'I hear Fox didn't last too long in Miami . . .'

Chin's slanted eyes narrowed even more. He pulled at his cigarette and looked straight at D. 'Well, maybe he made some enemies.'

'Or maybe he already had enemies, from before . . .?' D. suggested, returning the stare.

163

There was silence for a while, then Chin smiled and said: 'You seem to know something about that, D.?!'

D. shifted his position. Raising his eyebrows he said: 'Bwoy, to tell you the truth, Tony, I don't feel seh the Cubans dem have anything to do with dat . . .'

Chin looked thoughtful. When he spoke, his voice was noticeably colder. Almost as if he was speaking to himself.

'Imagine, a man work for years to establish his business, then he get into some problems and someone just comes and takes over his space.' He looked into D.'s eyes. 'How would you feel, man?'

It wasn't really a question. D. waited for Chin to continue but the man simply finished his cigarette and stubbed it out under his shoe. There was still something D. wanted to find out.

'So, I did t'ink seh ouno just swap territory,' he suggested.

Chin sighed heavily.

'That was what Skeets and the others said when I met with them after I got out. Since I couldn't operate freely in the States no more, I'd take over London from Fox and he would run Miami. I didn't like that, but I had no choice.' He paused, contemplating what had already happened. 'I don't really like it here. It's too far from Yard and it's difficult to get the merchandise in. In Miami, you can make much more money and faster.'

'I see what you mean,' D. said.

Chin looked at him, his head tilted sideways. 'So you think I ordered the hit on Fox, right?'

D. shrugged. 'It don't matter to me, Tony. The man probably set Blue on me, so . . .'

'You might not believe this, but I had nothing to do with it,' Chin continued. 'You see, Fox arrived in Miami with some of his soldiers and started reorganizing everything. He upset a lot of people I used to work with. While I was inside, my lieutenants kept the business going and everybody was happy. They had no intention to let an outsider come and take over. So you see, besides the Cubans, either my people or one of the Yankee gangs could have killed him.'

D. reflected on the story for a while. It sounded possible.

'So, what you gwan do now? Stay in London?'

Chin rubbed the back of his neck.

'That is what I wanted to see you about,' he said. 'You see, if I'm gonna make it work I need to rearrange certain things. Also, I had to bring in a few people from the States. Over here I don't know who to trust, it's a different scene.'

D. nodded silently.

'What I need is a few reliable soldiers around me, people with brains and guts, who know how things should run . . . people like you . . .'

Somehow, the offer didn't come as a surprise. Ever since he first met Chin that night at Joseph's house, D. knew that the man was sly. He began to understand why Chin was so feared.

'You know I got my own team, Tony. I'm doing fine and I got a good partner.'

'That is what I'm talking about, man. There are too many little outfits. What we need is one big operation . . . we could control every side of the trade in this town. Any man who gets his own supply would have to pay us dues to do business.'

Chin sounded really sure of himself. It hadn't gone unnoticed to D. that he used 'we' as if they had mutual interests in the plan. He thought for a moment . . . There was no point in refusing too hastily, that could be taken as disrespect.

165

'I appreciate the offer, seen?! And I know seh you have 'nough experience ina de business . . . Still I feel seh I should continue working with my people dem. I like the way t'ings ah run now,' D. answered after seemingly considering the proposition for a while. 'Money can't run like in Miami, but there is enough business for your team and mine,' he added, trying to offer a reasonable compromise. 'Any help you need, you just call me. I have good soldiers . . .'

Chin took his time to respond. He sighed and said almost casually, 'Well, that's all I really wanted to see you about. I thought you might want to be part of the *new order* . . .'

He stressed the last two words, as if they held a special meaning. D. reflected that there was no point in any further discussion. He had heard what Chin had to say.

'I'm going back downstairs, Tony. Remember; call me any time you need help.'

Chin was still leaning against the pillar, an indefinable look on his face. He lit a cigarette. D. started walking towards the exit. He was half-way there when he heard the voice behind him.

'D., this is an offer you can't refuse . . .'

Without breaking rhythm, D. spun round slowly. He looked straight into the slanted eyes fixing him through the smoke, a few yards away.

'You're threatening me, Tony?'

Chin let out a short, hollow laugh. He shrugged and grinned. 'I never threaten anyone. They might become my enemies . . .'

D. nodded and left. He knew a man like Chin was not to be taken lightly, but he didn't owe him anything. He went back to the balcony for Sticks and they walked down to meet the others.

166

You're sure it's the right flats?'

Slinga shifted in his seat impatiently. He and Pablo had sat in the car watching the entrance to the block for almost an hour.

'Yes, man. Just cool, him soon come . . .' Pablo answered reassuringly.

He switched on the wipers once more and peered through the windscreen into the darkness outside. Two silhouettes were coming out of the building and running towards one of the cars under the downpour. A heavy rain had been falling relentlessly for most of the day and the darkened sky had caused the night to fall even earlier than it usually did in winter. Gusts of cold wind were angrily lashing at the car windscreen. Pablo switched off the wipers and struck a match to light the spliff he had just finished building. He blew out the smoke, reflecting that there was a possibility that the man they were waiting for might not show up after all. Yet, he had reliable information that he would, so it was best to wait a little longer.

As if reading his thoughts, Slinga asked, 'So you feel seh dat gal tell the truth?'

'She knows the bwoy's baby mother, man. She tell her him due fe come see the youths dem today.'

Roy, the man they were waiting for, was a dealer who had worked for D.'s outfit for several months. He used to pay up more or less regularly until, a few weeks earlier, he suddenly disappeared. The word on the street was that

Roy was hooked and had smoked a fair amount of the crack himself. Now, with no way to repay his debt and fearing for his life, he had gone into hiding. D. had sent the two soldiers to try and recoup the money or, failing that, to execute sentence on Roy. He had to be made an example of to send a warning to the other dealers.

Pablo passed the spliff to Slinga, whose face was looking even sterner than usual. They spent another twenty minutes killing time, rocked by the hypnotic rhythm pattern of the raindrops merging with the beat of the music from the car speakers. Suddenly Pablo, who was keeping watch on the entrance to the flats, called out to his half-asleep companion, 'See him deh . . .!'

Slinga straightened up in his seat and focused on the door of the flats through which a tall silhouette had just disappeared. Pablo switched off the ignition and they left the car quickly, sprinting under the rain to catch up with their target. Once inside the hall, they stopped and listened. The sound of wet footsteps on the concrete stairs was clear enough in the silence of the flats. As quietly as possible, the two soldiers headed upstairs. They reached the second flight of steps just in time to glimpse Roy turning right onto the darkened landing.

They climbed up the few steps, staying close to the wall. The sound of keys clinking together was clearly audible a few yards away. Slowly, Pablo drew out the gun he carried under his jacket. Slinga's open knife was already in his hand. They didn't know whether Roy was armed or not but were not taking any chances. Cautiously, Slinga stuck out his head from behind the wall. Roy had just opened the door of a flat and was about to enter.

Swiftly, Slinga stepped on to the landing, Pablo right behind him. Just as Roy was turning to close the door behind him, he saw the two silhouettes lunging at him. He tried to push the door shut, but Slinga was already on him. Blocking the panel with his left foot, he threw himself forward and slashed with the knife. The sharpened blade caught Roy on the shoulder, cutting through his clothes and digging into his flesh. He cried out and lost balance as Pablo threw his weight against the door. His back up against the corridor wall, Roy saw the gun pointed at his head and froze. Slinga grabbed him by the collar and pushed the knife under his throat.

'One sound and you dead . . .!' he said coldly.

Quietly, Pablo closed the door of the flat. The attack had lasted less than a minute. The sound of a television was filtering through the door of the living room, visible behind the glass pane. Pablo looked at Roy.

'Who in deh?'

'Only my woman and the children . . .' The voice was hoarse.

His gun held low, Pablo opened the door and entered the living room. To the left, a young woman sat on a sofa holding a baby girl. Absorbed in the programme she was watching, she didn't notice Pablo until he was only two yards away from her. A young boy was sitting at her feet, eyes on the screen. She suddenly turned to the right and her eyes widened with surprise.

'Be quiet and everyt'ing will be al'right!' Pablo said calmly before she could speak.

She looked at him, then at the gun he held casually in his hand and nodded, clutching the baby girl tight against her. She was in her mid-twenties with close-cropped hair and large eyes. The little boy hadn't moved. He was looking at Pablo silently, more puzzled than afraid. Then Slinga came in, pushing a visibly shaken Roy in front of him. The girl turned towards him and gasped as she saw the dark, wet patch that marked his light-coloured jacket. She quickly controlled herself under Pablo's dark stare.

Slinga pulled out a wooden chair from behind the living room table and ordered his prisoner to sit down, shoving him roughly. While Pablo went to inspect the other rooms, he took the man's belt and tied his hands behind him tightly. Pablo came back and took a chair to sit right in front of Roy. 'You know why we come see you . . .' he stated flatly.

It wasn't a question. Roy nodded nervously and started to speak. Pablo lifted up the gun and pressed the barrel against the captive's chest, pushing hard. 'No baddah seh not'ing, bwoy! I tell you when to talk.'

Roy's forehead was shiny with beads of sweat. He managed to swallow, with some difficulty, his eyes on the gun. Pablo looked at him, grinning wickedly. 'Me did t'ink seh you lef' the country already, you know!'

From behind Roy, Slinga let out a mirthless laugh. 'You shoulda do dat, man . . .' he taunted him.

Still grinning Pablo turned towards the girl, sitting very still on the sofa. 'What's your name?'

She hesitated for a few seconds, then answered. 'Laura.'

'Well, Laura . . . your bwoyfriend owe we some money. We did trust him, but it look like him try fe rob we.'

Pablo's voice was calm, almost pleasant. He paused, then asked the girl, 'You know where the money is?'

Laura was breathing loudly. Pablo's piercing gaze was making her nervous and she could feel her hands shaking. She managed to answer. 'No . . . I don't know nothing . . .'

When he turned back to Roy, Pablo's grin had disappeared. 'So wha' you ah seh, bwoy? You have the cash . . .?'

Roy lifted up his face. There was no mercy in the cold eyes that stared into his. He began to speak, his voice trembling despite himself. 'I'll get the money . . . this week . . .'

Before he managed to finish his sentence, Pablo lifted up his right hand and whipped him across the face with the gun butt. The man's head jerked backwards under the blow. The pain was intense, but Roy stopped himself from crying out. He knew the mean reputation that followed D. and his outfit. If he showed any weakness, it would only incite them to more violence.

A trickle of blood was now visible on his lips, where the heavy gun had cut into the flesh. From behind, Slinga grabbed his hair and pulled his head upwards, forcing him to face Pablo.

'It look like we ha fe kill you today, bwoy!' he growled.

Roy's face was bathed in sweat, blood dripping down slowly from his mouth on to his clothes. He heaved a sigh, swallowed hard and said through tumescent lips: 'I have some money . . . here.'

'Weh it deh?' Pablo asked drily.

'In the other room, I'll get it for you.'

His hands still tied behind his back, Roy got up. Slinga pushed him back down on the chair. 'Make the girl get it!' he said.

'Laura,' Roy called out in a shaky voice. 'Go to the bedroom; there's a paper bag in the wardrobe, behind my clothes. Bring it . . .'

Laura looked at Pablo before getting up slowly, still holding the baby girl. She walked unsteadily across the room, followed by the little boy who was now too afraid to stay in the room with the men. Slinga went out behind

171

her. When they came back, he was holding a brown paper bag. He opened it and emptied the contents on the table, while Laura and her children went back to the sofa. Quickly, Slinga counted the bundle of notes. Holding the money, he looked at Pablo.

'Nine hundred pounds . . .' he said gloomily.

Pablo was silent for a few seconds reflecting on the situation. Then, shaking his head disapprovingly, he put the barrel of the gun against Roy's neck, pressing against his windpipe. 'You owe fifteen hundred pounds . . . Wha'ppen to the rest of the money?'

Roy forced himself to look at Pablo. 'I . . . some man have money for me . . . give me a little time. I'll get it . . . I swear.'

Pablo sighed. Quick as a flash, his left hand slapped Roy's face hard, jerking it sideways. 'Don't tell me no lie, bwoy!'

On the sofa, Laura whinged, quickly putting one hand on her mouth to stop herself. Once again, Roy managed to absorb the pain without a sound. His shoulder was aching horribly now, his lips were swollen and he could feel his head spinning. Breathing heavily, he pleaded: 'OK . . . I . . . I smoked a lot of the stuff. I've got a problem . . . But I'll get the money, I'll pay it back . . . Just give me a couple of days.'

Pablo stared at Roy for a while. He felt no compassion for the man, but it would serve no purpose to hurt him now. Better try to get back the rest of the money. He looked at Slinga, then back at Roy and said: 'You have until Saturday. Three days is plenty time.'

Through the pain, Roy managed to nod gratefully. He would have welcomed any reprieve, no matter how short, as long as they left him alive tonight. As if regretting his own generosity, Pablo added, 'Personally, I wouldn't mind kill you now and forget the money. Still, D. don't like to lose any cash . . .'

'I'll get it by Saturday, don't worry,' Roy said as convincingly as he could.

Pablo let out a dry laugh as he got up and walked towards the sofa. 'Worry? I don't worry.'

Gently, he caressed the baby girl's hair. Looking straight into Laura's eyes, he said: 'If you don't have the money by Saturday, I'll leave you alive . . . but you'll have to bury someone.'

There was no anger in Pablo's voice and barely a hint of threat. Yet Roy knew it was no bluff. He didn't answer.

'Come, star, mek we leff yah!' Pablo told Slinga.

After a last look around the room, the two men walked out slowly.

'See you later, Roy,' Slinga said casually, before closing the door of the flat.

Downstairs, the rain was still pouring down on the silent parking lot. They ran to the car. Once inside, Pablo switched on the engine, changed the cassette on the stereo, and rolled a spliff. He looked at his watch and swore. It was much too late for the date he had made with a girl earlier that day. He shrugged, realizing that he felt hungry.

'I coulda eat somet'ing, yes,' Slinga answered when Pablo asked him.

The rain beating down on the windscreen, Pablo drove the car through the dark, glistening streets. With a little luck, they might make it to the restaurant on the front line before it closed.

The phone in one hand, Charlie got up and turned down the volume of the stereo. Sitting in an armchair in front of the television, Indian noticed the frown on his friend's

173

face. Charlie didn't sit back down. Donna was on the line, her voice shaking with mixed emotions as she delivered the bad news.

'Arrest him for what?' Charlie asked.

'Dem seh murder . . . and rape.'

Charlie looked down at Indian, shaking his head. He tried to reassure Donna but found it difficult to sound convincing. After telling her to keep calm and wait for him to call back, he hung up.

'Is wha' happ'n?' Indian asked.

Charlie was still standing up, a look of deep concentration etched across his face. Finally, he sat back down on the sofa and sighed.

'D. got arrested.'

Indian said nothing. He waited for Charlie to continue.

Charlie took a swig from the beer he had been sipping when the phone call came in. Slowly, he repeated what Donna had told him. Three plainclothes police officers had come to the flat around six o'clock that morning with a warrant for D.'s arrest. They had quite literally caught him sleeping and barely gave him time to get dressed before they took him away. One of the detectives said that D. would be charged for murder and rape. Donna had tried to contact Charlie straight away, but he and Indian had been on the move since early morning and his mobile phone was out of order. She had called D.'s lawyer who said that he would go to the station at once.

'The lawyer must get him off, man. Dem don't have no evidence.' Indian tried to sound optimistic.

'I don't know . . .' Charlie sounded gloomy. 'If they get a warrant, they must have something.'

The two men were silent for a while, each trying to figure out how serious the situation was. Charlie finished his beer. He looked at the clock on the wall. Almost noon.

There was a slim chance that the police might be bluffing. Maybe they were just trying to trick D. into confessing to whatever they wanted to charge him with. Charlie knew that wouldn't work. But if they didn't let him go soon, they had to have something.

'Dem cyan make the murder charge stick. Dem don't have no witness,' Indian said thoughtfully. 'What about dat rape business?'

'Blue's girl would have to testify in court against him.'

Indian laughed drily. 'Testify? She's not crazy . . . Anyhow she talk, she's dead and she knows dat.'

Charlie didn't answer. Indian was right. The girl knew that testifying against D. was like committing suicide. Yet there was something deeply disturbing about the story, something he couldn't quite figure out. The sound of footsteps on the stairs drew him out of his meditation. Marcus was making his way down, followed by his mother and Sweetie. They had gone shopping earlier on, now Charmaine was about to fix some lunch.

'Charlie, wha'ah gwan?' Sweetie sat on the sofa beside her cousin while Charmaine went to the kitchen with Marcus.

'Cool, you know . . .' Charlie answered evasively.

Sweetie looked at the two men with prying eyes. Charlie seemed preoccupied and even the usually placid Indian had a serious expression.

'Somet'ing wrong?' Sweetie asked.

'Just a little problem . . . We'll take care of it, Sis,' Charlie muttered, trying to sound dismissive.

He always called Sweetie 'Sis'. They had spent their early years together back in Jamaica, growing up in their grandmother's house in Spanish Town. Since Sweetie was two years older than he, Charlie had always seen her as his older sister and still did. The trouble was that it was

175

very hard for him to hide anything from Sweetie. She was terribly inquisitive by nature, and even more so with Charlie.

'Build a spliff now . . .' Charlie pointed to the engraved wooden box on the coffee table.

Sweetie paused before helping herself to what she needed from the box. The television was still on but no one was watching it. From the kitchen, the sound of plates and pans was coming through. Sweetie finished building her spliff and lit it. After a few pulls, she turned to Indian, watching him attentively. It was hard for him to ignore the stare.

'Wait! Wha' me do you?' he asked, half smiling.

'Is why you look so sad today, man?' Sweetie returned the smile.

Indian had known her for a long time too. He knew she wouldn't stop asking questions until she got answers. Still, he wasn't the one to decide on this.

'Me cyan say not'ing, Sweetie. No disrespect.'

Undeterred, Sweetie turned to Charlie, eyebrows raised.

'Al'right, since you must know; D. got arrested.'

Sweetie frowned through the smoke. She sat there silently while Charlie told her all he knew about it.

'What evidence dem have?' Sweetie asked after listening to the story.

'Ah dat we trying to find out,' Indian said.

The room was quiet for several minutes. Then Sweetie started: 'So . . . dat girl . . . must have agreed to testify against D.; else dem couldn't charge him.'

Charlie shook his head dubiously. 'She must know she can't get away with it.'

Sweetie took a pull from the spliff. 'Al'right; if dem

don't have no evidence and no witness for the murder, why charge him with dat as well ?'

Charlie rubbed the back of his neck. There was a connection somewhere, he could feel it. As if talking to himself, he said: 'D. raped the girl to smoke Blue out, right? So . . . if she testify for that, they can prove that D. was looking for Blue. That means he's the main suspect for the murder.'

Charlie stopped and reflected on the logic of it all. It started to look disturbingly likely that this was the way the police were operating. He was about to say something, when Sweetie interrupted him.

'Wait! I knew there was something, but I couldn't remember what.'

Charlie and Indian looked at the girl. She paused, collecting her thoughts before continuing. 'Last week . . . Thursday or Friday, one ah dem nights, I go High Noon with some friends. Now hear dis! Guess who me see down deh . . .?'

Sweetie stopped. Charlie and Indian were looking at her expectantly. This was no time for games, Sweetie could see that. She let out: 'Dat same girl . . . whe' she name? Rita!'

'So what?' Charlie asked impatiently.

'Hold on! I bet ouno cyan guess who she did spar with . . .'

The two men waited as Sweetie held back for a moment.

'Talk nah, man!' Indian pressed her.

Sweetie looked at Charlie. 'Chin,' she said simply.

The name floated in the air, as if echoing through the room. After what seemed like a long silence, Charlie's voice repeated, almost despite himself.

177

'Chin . . .'

'Chin set her up to testify against D.!' Indian said, incredulous.

Charlie could feel a deep, cold anger welling inside him. D. had told him about Chin's offer at the show and the veiled threat when he had refused it. Even so, it was hard to believe that a man could be that devious. Yet again, anything could be expected from Tony Chin.

At that point, Charmaine walked in from the kitchen. 'Anybody hungry?' she asked lightly.

Three pairs of eyes turned towards her. Puzzled, she looked at each in turn. She didn't see hunger there, but she could sense various emotions. Charmaine took a closer look at Charlie. There was something on his face that she couldn't quite define, but it frightened her.

Another win! A contented grin on his face, Sticks nodded to Lloyd before heading for the counter. It was the third race in a row in which he had placed a winning bet. By contrast, it was a rotten day for Lloyd, who crumpled the paper slip in his hand before throwing it in a bin. The two had arrived at the betting shop early that afternoon and spent several hours trying their luck. Though Lloyd had won small amounts, he had consistently been denied success on his more substantial bets and, all in all, had lost just under £200. Having collected his earnings, Sticks came back. Now £500 richer, he had wisely decided it was enough luck for one day.

'Rest it now, man. Today is not your day,' he told his friend.

Lloyd knew Sticks was right; a good gambler has to know when to quit. He wasn't so much worried about the money. Lloyd was a dealer and £200 was a small amount of money to him. Rather, he was upset by the fact that only his smallest bets had been successful and he had been unable to make anything back for his big losses. He shrugged.

'Come, star, mek we get some food.'

They walked out of the bookie's shop. Outside, the cold wind slapped them as they stepped on to the already darkened street. It was still only around six o'clock, but night fell early in the winter season. Sticks gathered his jacket collar around his neck. The restaurant was right across from the bookie. Winners and losers always ended up there.

Lloyd and Sticks crossed the road and entered the restaurant. The place was busy and warm and the smell of cooked food teased their hungry stomachs. After they placed their orders, they started talking with some friends who had left the betting shop earlier, each one commenting on their gambling day. Once their meals were ready, Sticks got one of the men sitting at a table to make room for him, while Lloyd ate at one of the narrow shelves set against the wall for that purpose. The atmosphere inside the restaurant was noisy, music and loud discussions merging to create a deafening background noise. Most of the front line regulars were there at this time of the evening, dinner time. Lloyd had barely finished his meal when he was approached by a short man wrapped in an oversized sheepskin coat, looking for a deal. The man waited, nervously shifting from one foot to the other, and glancing furtively around the room while Lloyd ate the last of the stew. Once he had finished, he belched and headed for the toilets. The man soon followed him.

With a satisfied smile, Sticks disposed of his empty plate and shouted at G.B. standing behind his counter: 'Wicked food, my boss!'

He sat back and continued his debate with a youth about the eventual outcome of the heavyweight boxing match to be broadcast later that night. Sticks was putting across his point in favour of Mike Tyson, when the voice reached him.

'Eh, Scarface! What's happening?'

Aware that he was the one being addressed, Sticks stopped in mid-sentence and looked up in the direction of the voice. A man was standing a few yards away, near the door, grinning at him. Squinting, Sticks stared at him for a few seconds. Only an enemy would call him Scarface. Across the room, conversations stopped, all eyes turned towards the newcomer. Sticks took his time to answer . . . For the man to come and insult him on his own territory he either had to have a death wish or be totally insane. There was something familiar about the face. The man was dark, stout in build, and wearing a coat.

Slowly, he walked towards Sticks, his hands in his coat pockets, still grinning. Just as he stopped, only a yard or so away from him, Sticks remembered. Bare-headed and without his dark glasses, he looked a little different, but it was the same man who had stood in their way at the Reggae Awards show a few months earlier. Chin's Yankee soldier . . .

'You nah have no business 'round yah, bwoy. Go back whe' you come from . . .' Sticks hissed scornfully.

Everyone in the restaurant was watching. Music was still playing in the background, but the atmosphere was now heavy. Sticks was a known short-tempered youth, and D.'s right-hand man. No man in his right mind would dare to come trouble him without a good reason, and a solid back-up. The man had to be brave . . .

Oblivious to the apparent danger he was in, the man said: 'I'm just buying some food, man.'

He was still grinning. Sticks got up slowly, his hands hanging loose by his sides. He felt totally cold inside. At that moment, Lloyd walked back in from the toilet and froze like everyone else. Sticks was the only one from the outfit in the restaurant but several of the youths there would only be too happy to prove themselves and help him out.

'You nah buy not'ing in here, so leave now while you can,' Sticks spat out icily.

The man stared at Sticks for a few short, tense seconds, then nodded. 'OK, I'm going. But remember, we're taking over . . . your posse is out of the game, man.'

Sticks felt a tingle at the back of his neck as he recalled the conversation he had had with Charlie a few days earlier. They had all agreed that no one who was involved in setting D. up would get away with it. His right hand slipped slowly behind his back. At the same time, he saw the man take a few steps back, his hands still in his pockets and heard G.B.'s voice from behind. 'Sticks! Not in here . . .'

The man had his back against the door now. 'Easy, man. We'll meet again . . .'

His face was straight, without fear. Carefully, he took his left hand out of his pocket, reached for the handle and opened the door, his eyes still on Sticks. Without another word, he walked out to a white Mercedes parked in front of the restaurant, engine still running. Through the half-opened car window, Sticks thought he recognized the other Yankee soldier from the show that night. He sat back down. Slowly the conversations started back.

'Who is this?' Lloyd asked after a while.

Sticks didn't answer him. He felt a cold anger in the pit of his stomach. In a sense, he almost regretted not settling the score there and then. He picked up his drink from the table and finished it. The man was right about one thing, they would meet again.

Leroy stretched and picked up the television remote control from the table. He switched between channels, but found nothing of interest to him. Sitting beside him, Cindy was busy with her colouring book. She had not left her uncle's side since he arrived earlier that evening and had even insisted on eating her dinner by his side. Leroy had returned from Jamaica two days earlier, having stayed a week longer than planned. He had found Donna still in shock from D.'s arrest, but there was little he could do to comfort her. D.'s case was bad and she knew it. Even Cindy wasn't her normal buoyant self. She had witnessed D.'s arrest the previous week and kept asking why the police had taken him away and when he would be back. Donna didn't want to lie to her daughter yet the truth was hard to explain to a child.

Donna had listened keenly to Leroy as he gave her news of family and friends back home. She could feel the change in her brother, the way he looked relaxed, still glowing from the hot Caribbean sun. Sitting by him, she could almost hear the voices of people milling around in the heat of the streets and smell the scent of the mellow Kingston nights. After hearing her uncle's colourful stories, Cindy had made her mother promise that she would take her there, next year . . .

Yet Leroy had found that Kingston especially had changed a lot, for the worse. The part of town where he had grown as a youngster was now more difficult than ever to survive in. In his time, despite the deprivation, or probably because of it, there was a special quality to ghetto life. Traditionally, the various areas that constituted downtown Kingston were tightly knit communities where people looked out for each other. Even in the roughest parts, the 'leaders', residents with influence and muscle, would generally protect their communities against outside threats. At the height of elections, when the nominal political allegiances of the various areas of downtown Kingston were divided in favour of one or other of the two parties, PNP (Socialist) or JLP (Labour), turned into mindless violence, these unofficial community leaders effectively became warlords. They would set up defence systems to protect their areas against outside attacks and organize and direct the gangs of gun-toting youths that raided enemy territory. Of course there were disputes and heated arguments between neighbours also, but these were usually settled peacefully. In this respect, Kingston was a totally different place now.

'Hey, Donna,' Leroy called out. 'You 'member Willy, from First Avenue?'

Donna came in from the kitchen and sat on a chair. 'Little Willy? Yeah, man. Me an' him used to go school together.'

'Well, Willy deh ah GP right now, fe murder.'

'Weh you ah seh? Willy?! A youth who was so quiet and nice?'

Leroy laughed. 'Him turn bad bwoy! Dem seh him did run drugs for some man. One night two youths try fe rob him outside one bar. Willy jus' draw out him gun and shoot the two ah dem ina the head, one bullet each . . .'

Donna shook her head sadly. At school, Willy was one of the best behaved and hardest working students. How did he become a gun man?

"Nough youths deh a jail fe murder, you know,' Leroy explained. 'Me ah tell you; Kingston's like the Wild West. And the worst about it is dat it's the young ones dem who do most of the shooting. Imagine dat – fourteen-year-old youths ah carry gun regular now.'

'So what about the police dem?'

Leroy looked at his sister. 'Police?! Anything ah run in Jamaica, police ina it. Anyway, right now the bad bwoys dem shoot down police too and feel no way. Ah so t'ings run ah Yard.'

All this sounded really crazy to Donna. Growing up in Kingston, she got used to the violence that occasionally surfaced but not the kind of lawlessness Leroy was talking about. Leroy was silent for a while. He looked down at Cindy, seemingly absorbed in her book, before adding, 'I wouldn't live down deh now . . . not in town anyway.'

'Wait! You was a bad man too . . .' Donna teased him.

'I was rough, yes. But I make a difference between standing for your rights and robbing and killing for greed,' Leroy answered. 'The way t'ings ah run now, a man life don't worth not'ing. Even in your own area, if a man grudge you for your car, your girl, anyt'ing you have, even your house, him will kill you an' take it from you.'

Donna knew Leroy spoke the truth. All her friends who had gone back had told her the same thing. Within herself she wanted to hold on to the vision of the town she had left behind, the way it was then . . . She looked at Leroy thoughtfully.

'All dem man deh, it's drugs mash dem up.'

'Drugs, yes! But hear dis: if you grow up poor in Jamaica, with no education, drugs is the only t'ing that will take you out of the trap. Either you take a chance or you stay and suffer.'

'Wickedness . . .' Donna said gloomily. 'Look how many ah we dead or in jail t'rough dis t'ing. You can never win.'

Leroy didn't answer right away. He observed his sister

184

in silence, he could feel her distress. He leaned over and said softly: 'There is not'ing you can do about D. now, only get strong again and live upright, D. knew the risks, that's the way he lives.'

'He is not a bad person, you know Leroy. He always treated me and Cindy nice.' Donna's voice reflected her anguish.

'I know dat, and I don't hold not'ing against him. But D. grow up downtown and him know seh the only way out of the ghetto, out of poverty, is the rough way. Him make up him mind a long time ago – it's too late for him to change now.'

Donna sighed and rested her head against the back of the chair. Leroy was right. She had to be strong and go on living the way she did before. There was no point torturing herself by hoping. Yet deep inside, she knew the feeling she had for D., that bond which had brought them back together after all those years, would stay alive. She saw her brother smile at her and forced herself to wipe away the frown from her face. Gently, Donna placed her left hand over her stomach. At that moment she made a silent vow that no matter how long it took, D. would one day see the child she was carrying for him.

extracts reading groups
competitions books new
discounts extracts events
competitions extracts extracts reading groups
books new discounts
events books reading groups
reading groups extracts extracts
extracts new books new
interviews reading groups
events extracts extracts
discounts events books
new books events
events new interviews
discounts extracts discounts books

www.panmacmillan.com

extracts events reading groups
competitions books extracts new